D0966146

LOVE WORTH FINDING

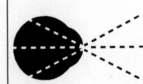

This Large Print Book carries the
Seal of Approval of N.A.V.H.

LOVE WORTH FINDING

A SUN-KISSED ROMANCE

CATHY MARIE HAKE

THORNDIKE PRESS

A part of Gale, Cengage Learning

GALE
CENGAGE Learning™

Detroit • New York • San Francisco • New Haven, Conn • Waterville, Maine • London

GALE
CENGAGE Learning

LIBRARY OF CONGRESS CATALOGING-IN-PUBLICATION DATA

Hake, Cathy Marie.
    Love worth finding / by Cathy Marie Hake. — Large print ed.
        p. cm. — (A star-kissed romance San Diego; bk. 3)
    (Thorndike Press large print Christian fiction)
    ISBN-13: 978-1-4104-2754-0
    ISBN-10: 1-4104-2754-4
    1. Large type books. I. Title.
PS3608.A5454L684 2010
813'.6—dc22   2010014472

Published in 2010 by arrangement with Barbour Publishing, Inc.

LOVE WORTH FINDING

ONE

Brandon Stevens spied his target and broke out in a cold sweat. He'd completed over a hundred missions, but none had ever affected him like this one. As a Navy SEAL, he'd done demolition work, rescues, reconnaissance . . . but of all the places he'd been, none ever seemed this foreign. The map in his pocket had proven to be accurate, so he hoped this would be one of those in-and-out operations that went off without a hitch.

A detailed sweep of the area showed little activity. Good. He slid out of the jeep, strode determinedly toward the entrance, and spotted his target behind the glass door. The minute he stepped inside, a motion detector went off.

It played "Here Comes the Bride."

For an instant, Brandon almost yielded to the temptation to bolt. Instead, he resolutely stepped forward to stop the stupid thing from pealing that song. His athletic shoes sank into the deep plush carpeting the color of a Bazooka — the bubble gum, not the weapon. Silvery mirrors reflected billows of satin, lace, and fluff. Sensing a presence, he wheeled to the side.

"Welcome to Della's." A shapely woman rose from behind a mannequin and smoothed the shoulder of the tuxedo it wore. "May I help you?"

"Yeah. Gloves. I need gloves."

"This way, please." Her dark brown hair flowed in a cascade of curls clear down to her waist as she pivoted toward a gleaming display case.

"Military, marriage, magician, or mime?" She looked at him expectantly. A man could get lost in her deep chocolate eyes.

"Milit— oh, no. They're not for me." He crammed his hand into the rear pocket of his jeans and yanked out a piece of paper. Smoothing out the crinkles, he read, "Size six, elbow-length, white satin gloves."

She beamed at him. "It's always so nice when a man knows what his bride wants."

"No, no. That's not it. They're for my niece."

Laughter bubbled out of the woman. "Someone's going to owe you a big favor for running this errand."

"No kidding!" He grinned back at her.

"The school play opens tonight. My niece is Cinderella, and my sister-in-law can only find one of the gloves."

"Mindy Stevens!"

"How did you know?" He held up a hand. "No, don't tell me. She probably got that fancy blue gown from over there." He cast a glance at the far wall of the shop where racks held a veritable rainbow of gowns.

"Yes. Here. Size six." Drawing a pair of shimmering gloves from a box, the gal laid them across the case. "They're washable satin, so Mindy'll be able to use them later for the prom."

"If they can find them," Brandon said in a wry tone.

A frown creased her face.

"That didn't come out right." Brandon prized loyalty, and he'd just made a flippant remark, which could be misconstrued. "Annette's doing a great job with Mindy. It's not easy for her, everything considered."

The sales gal shook her head. "The stitching on the hem of these is flawed."

"Not a problem. The audience won't see that." He reached for the gloves. So did the woman. Stubborn little thing wouldn't let go.

"I sell only the best." She tugged.

"I'm in a hurry." He pulled. For all the

9

missions he'd been on, the battles he'd fought, this one rated as the strangest — a ridiculous tug o' war over a slippery woman's glove! "Listen, lady, just sell it to me."

"Absolutely not." She grabbed hold of the glove with her other hand, too. "I refuse to take advantage of you."

"You're cheating." He tapped her left hand.

"Two gloves, two hands." Merriment danced in her eyes as she tried to tow the gloves closer to herself. The satin didn't allow her much of a grip.

Tightening his hold on the fabric fingers and twisting for better grip and traction, Brandon could feel her losing the battle.

"You're fighting for something you don't even value."

"Wrong. I value family. Mindy needs these."

"These are smudged and wrinkled." She let go.

Brandon scowled — first at her then at the limp, crumpled white fabric.

"I have more in the back room. Please give me a minute."

Brandon watched her walk away and set the ruined gloves on the display case. She'd better have another pair. The small town of Granite Cliff didn't have anywhere else that would carry fripperies like this. His sister-in-law had been in a full-on, tears-in-her-eyes dither when she begged him to go out and buy gloves for Mindy. A silver anniversary cruise resulted in Annette's unexpected pregnancy, and Brandon would rather be caught in enemy territory without a weapon than deal with upsetting a forty-five-year-old woman with morning sickness. Come to think of it, he *was* in hostile territory without a weapon. . . .

"Excuse me." The clerk peeped at him from behind a curtain leading to the back room. "How tall are you?"

The only time in his life that his height had been an issue was when he wanted to join the SEALs. They didn't have an official height requirement, but a more compact build was definitely the norm. "Six foot. Why?"

"I wouldn't normally ask, but you're in a hurry. I could go next door to the pet shop and borrow a ladder —"

"Say no more." He strode to the storeroom. "Point the way."

She motioned toward the top of a well-organized series of shelves. "Top tier, second row from the left, third box."

"Third box up, or third box down?" He headed back toward the goal.

"Both, actually, if you don't mind. I'd like a backup in case there's another flawed glove."

"Good thinking." His shoulder pulled as he reached upward. Brandon gritted his teeth against the pain. Stupid rotator cuff. The surgeon stated it would never be the same — and that cost him his place with the SEALs. "Here."

"Wonderful. Thank you so much!"

As she walked ahead of him to the register out front, Brandon resisted the urge to sweep his hand through her hair. She'd backed into something and had tinsey bits of shimmering stuff winking at him from those luscious curls.

"Thank you for shopping at Della's." Though that was her customary line when handing a patron the purchase, Della couldn't resist adding, "I'd normally say, 'Come back again,' but I have a funny feeling you'd rather be shot."

A deep laugh rumbled out of the hunk as he accepted the gloves. "I've been shot more than once. This was less painful."

"I'll take that as a compliment."

"You do that, ma'am." His *ringless* hand dwarfed the pale pink and silver bag, and his head tilted back. He sniffed. "Besides, this place smells a whale of a lot better than a hospital." A rakish grin crossed his rugged features, transforming somber, gunmetal gray eyes into pools of silver. He winked. "And you can take that as a compliment, too."

The wedding chime to the door sounded as he left. Della leaned against the counter and sighed. "Now why can't I order one of those for me? Tall, dark, handsome . . . deep voice, rough hands, great sense of humor, loves his family."

She straightened the business cards in the sterling holder and looked around. Five years after opening her bridal shop, she still loved her job — but every once in a while, she suffered a few pangs. This was one of those days. A friend had just come in, thrilled to tell her all about last night's romantic supper and marriage proposal. Della loved hearing all the details. Once again, Della received the honor of being invited to serve as a bridesmaid. Selling the bridal gown, bridesmaids' gowns, and arranging for all the announcements, etc. would bring in a tidy sum for the shop, too. All told, it was fabulous news.

Except for the fact that all of the Mr. Rights are getting snapped up, and I'm not interested in Mr. Leftover.

The door chimed again. Vanessa Adams from Whiskers, Wings, and Wags next door tugged on the hem of her bright red T-shirt. "I'm running over to Pudgy's for a sandwich. Did you want me to bring anything back for you?"

A low-calorie fruit salad in the refrigerator awaited her. Feeling the need to be self-indulgent, Della cast caution to the wind. "Want to share a mile-high pastrami?"

Vanessa laughed. "Sure."

"Oh! While you're there, will you please grab their catering brochure?"

"I didn't know they had one."

"They do. I'm putting together a wedding reception for someone who wants to do it like a giant picnic." She didn't mention the catering company the bride chose just went belly-up, so Della volunteered to make all-new, last minute arrangements. Navigating through disasters while making everything seem effortless was just part of the business.

"A picnic? Really?"

Della smiled. "No one makes better potato salad than Pudgy's."

"*Mmm.* I'll pick up a pint of it now, and we can . . . uh . . . taste test it. Yeah." Vanessa gave her a sassy grin. "That's it. Taste test it. Just to be sure they haven't changed the recipe, you know."

"Oh, the things I suffer for the sake of my patrons!" Della giggled. "In fact, a new company contacted me this morning — a confectioner. They have all sorts of decadent things like mint truffles, candied almonds —"

"As your friend and retail neighbor, it's my duty to help you taste test them, right?"

Della tapped a finger on her chin. "I'll have to think about it. As I recall, the only samples you get are pet food. I'm afraid you'll reciprocate!"

Vanessa groaned. "You heard about that?"

"About what?"

"My son thought the doggie chews were beef jerky. I caught him with a half-eaten piece yesterday."

"Oh, no!"

"Yeah, and my husband was no help at all. Nathan hooted about it then asked Jeff how it tasted. I told him if he took a bite, I wouldn't kiss him for a week."

"As if you'd ever carry out that threat." Della shook her head. Van and Nathan were married just a year and a half ago. They were head-over-heels in love, and Della often saw them together on the baseball team. They called themselves a match made in heaven, and Della had to agree — they

15

were one of the happiest couples she knew, and Vanessa adored Nathan's little son.

Della had been a bridesmaid in that wedding, too.

"Nathan's minding the store for me now. You'll notice I didn't suggest roast beef sandwiches."

"That's so gross!"

"You're being prissy again." Vanessa laughed. "Have you ever actually gotten dirty?"

"I've gotten hungry. Are you going to stand there, talking all day, or are you going to get the pastrami?"

Vanessa left, and Della spritzed cleaner on a case and polished the glass. She didn't mind Vanessa teasing her. Vanessa loved her for being just who she was. Their friendship started back in high school when Vanessa played the zany mascot and Della received the homecoming crown.

Growing up in a home like hers, Della didn't have a chance to be anything other than prissy. When she was less than a year old, her mother died. Her dad and two older brothers made a pact not to fall into the trap of turning her into a tomboy. As a result, she'd been their little princess — with enough frills, lace, and pink to smother a multitude of girls.

16

Daddy and the boys would go fishing and send her off to Miss Mannerly's Etiquette weekend. She took flute and piano lessons while her brothers tore up the lawn playing tackle football and practicing golf swings. The one "girly" thing she welcomed was dating — but they'd made utter pests of themselves and scared off most of the men after the first date.

Thanks to her overprotective brothers, the closest she would ever come to a groom was right now — when she fixed the mannequin's cuff links.

Two

"*Mmm.* She's a beaut." Brandon whistled. "Do you know how old she is?"

"Not sure." Nathan Adams pulled to a stop. "She's pretty tacky. What do you think?"

Brandon continued to stare at the ornate building. "I want her." Hopping out of the truck, he started thinking aloud. "We'll need a safety inspection first — she's made it through several earthquakes, so the foundation may have shifted. Assuming the foundation's safe, all the wood will have to be termited as soon as we pull off anything that's not salvageable." Even in his enthusiasm, Brandon meticulously noted each hazard and knew precisely where Nathan moved. "We'll need to contact Jim Martinez about supplying us with reproduction gingerbread and hardware."

"I already commissioned the foundation survey — I wouldn't pursue the project if there were problems with it."

"Great. Let's take a look inside."

"We have clearance, but there's no key."

"As if that matters." Brandon hustled up the stairs and quickly jimmied the lock. When his boss crooked a brow, Brandon chuckled. "Your tax dollars paid for that training."

Floor by floor, they walked through the old, rambling building. "Looks like it started out as a hotel then turned into a boarding house." Nathan stared out from a gabled window on the third floor. "I was thinking it would make a great bed-and-breakfast sort of place."

Brandon nodded. "The downstairs is cramped. Knock down a few walls, and you'll have big spaces that'd be great meeting or reception rooms. It'll be a good investment. Rent the place out for weddings and business seminars."

"My plate's already full with the high school expansion." Nathan turned. "Do you want this project?"

"Yep."

"One condition." Nathan locked eyes with him. "You're to be the brains, not the brawn. You have carte blanche to make decisions regarding architectural alterations, landscape, and decorating — but I'll fire you on the spot if you lift anything heavier than a hammer."

Brandon snapped off a salute. "Sir, yes, sir."

"Now that's the kind of training my tax dollars can go for."

Brandon knocked the edge of his fist against a doorframe. "Someone did a slap-dash job on repairs. I'm going to want to yank out the garbage and do it right."

His boss studied the window frame. "Re-placing the woodwork with Victorian mold-ings won't be cheap."

"Nope. But you can have it done right, or you can have it done right now." Brandon wanted this job so badly, he could taste it — but only if he could do a quality retrofit. He stared at his boss. "I do things right."

Nathan nodded. "That's why I offered you the job." He headed back down the stairs. "By the way — I already signed the papers for the property. You can start assembling a team."

"Hoo-ah!" Brandon passed Nathan on the stairs and shot him a look over his shoulder. "That's military, too."

"Why do I have the feeling you're going to import a bunch of your SEAL buddies to do the grunt work?"

"Don't I wish. They do it right. First time.

Every time." He shook his head. "Can't, though. Training schedule's a bear. I could probably round up some Seabees who just got out. They're great."

"Can't argue with that. I've got another reason I'm okay with it, too."

Brandon shot him a quick look. Nathan's tone warned he'd be delivering unwelcome news.

"The high school expansion is on a tight schedule. You'll be working with a skeleton crew, and I plan to pull them from your site on a few key dates."

"Good planning can make up for that — especially on a site this small."

Nathan paused on the last step. "I do everything aboveboard. Nothing under the table."

Most of the construction businesses in the area employed "day labor" which consisted of undocumented workers from across the border who were paid cheap wages that didn't show on the records. Doing so kept down the costs on a project, but it was illegal. Brandon hadn't risked his life serving his country for the past six years only to turn a blind eye to its laws. "Every man on the site is on the book. Wouldn't have it any other way."

"Good. Since that's out of the way, I have

21

something important to discuss."

"Important, huh?"

"Think that shoulder of yours would let you play baseball?"

After the surgery, the doctor told Brandon it would be six months before he'd recover. Within three months, Brandon exceeded every goal the physical therapist set. Even then, they still gave him a medical discharge. He could have fought it, but it boiled down to whether his pride was more important than his team members' safety. Brandon made the only possible decision. He'd been lucky to fall into a job that he enjoyed with a decent boss.

He resisted the urge to rub away a twinge along his incision. "I do what I want. I don't consult my shoulder."

"No use overtaxing it, though."

Brandon walked around a rotting area on the floor. "Back to talking about taxes? No way. So what's this about baseball?"

"Church league. We're down a few players, and —"

"Forget it. I'm not the church type."

"You don't have to be a member of the church to play. We have a couple other players who don't attend services. No pressure — it's just for fun and fellowship."

"Fun, yes — but the fellowship part

sounds touchy-feely."

"Nope. It's more like a prayer at the outset then grilled hot dogs before a game or ice cream afterward. Real low-key. Why don't you come tomorrow evening and give it a try? If you don't like it, or if your shoulder bothers you, you can walk away with no commitment, no questions asked."

"One time. No strings."

"Supper's on!" Della thumped the biggest pot in the house onto the table and glanced over her shoulder.

Footsteps sounded on the porch; then the screen door banged shut. "I'm coming. Whatever it is, give me doubles. I'm starving." Daddy sniffled loudly. "It smells like lasagna."

"Spaghetti."

"Triples."

"Me, too." Justin plopped into a chair. "And no skimping on the meatballs!"

Shoving a pitcher of iced tea into Gabe's hands, Della scoffed, "Since when have you guys gone hungry?"

Daddy brushed a kiss on her cheek. "We're still making up for all the years when you didn't know how to cook." He grabbed the basket of garlic bread and headed for the table.

Della looked at her family and felt an odd twang. Her brothers had moved into an apartment four years ago, but they still came home for supper Monday through Thursday. Weekends, they dated or fended for themselves. She'd love to have a place of her own, too — but Daddy would be so lonesome by himself in the house. She'd taken a big loan to start her business, so it made sense for her to stay at home.

I'm tired of being sensible.

"You'd better get over here, Sis." Sauce-laden noodles slithered across the tabletop as Gabe served himself. "Justin's going to eat the rest if you don't dive in."

"Go ahead, Justin." Della slipped into her chair. "Here. Have more garlic bread, too."

Justin stopped mid-bite and gave her a horrified look. "Oh, no. No. Not a chance."

"You don't want more garlic bread?" she asked oh-so-innocently.

"I'm wise to you. You can't pull that stunt on me twice. I said it once, and I'll say it 'til my dying day, no. Got that? I'm not going to put on one of those fancy monkey suits you rent out and get saddled into another show."

"Oh, Justin." Della gave him a disappointed look. "Why not? You look outstanding in a tux."

24

"Yeah, and three of the models gave you their telephone numbers," Gabe teased.

"That's just the problem." Justin made a disgusted sound. "Every last one of them thought just because we met at a bridal show that the date was supposed to get them back into one of those gowns again — and I'm not talking about getting another job modeling. Ten minutes into a date, and every one of them started talking about marriage."

"What's wrong with marriage?" Thoroughly disgruntled, Della glowered at him.

"Nothing — as long as it's someone else's," Gabe said. He took a long gulp of his tea. "And count me in with Justin — I'm not gonna play model groom for you, either."

Her dad drummed his fingers on the table. "When's the show, Princess?"

"Monday, the eighteenth. It's a luncheon in San Diego."

He nodded. "Power Electric is happy to supply you with men." He shot his sons a telling look. "Two of them."

Justin muttered, "Spare us the family-sticks-together speech, Dad. I should have known you'd pull rank on us."

"Talk about rank —" Gabe popped a whole meatball into his mouth and kept speaking. "Could you believe that skunk at the Java and Jelly? Whew!"

The conversation zipped all over the place, and Della didn't say much. She'd be interrogated to the *nth* degree if she confessed the scent she remembered from her day of work was left by a hunky young military man who bought gloves. He'd worn some kind of aftershave that lingered in the shop and left her inhaling deeply for the next hour.

"Earth to Della." Justin's voice registered.

"Oh — huh?" She shook herself.

"I said, since I'm going to have to strut around in that penguin suit for you, you have to help me with my billings tomorrow night. I'm behind."

Della shook her head. "I've got a game tomorrow night."

"When are you going to stop that and start dating?" Her father shook more Parmesan cheese on his plate. "I want my daughter walking down the aisle, not walking with crutches."

"If I get married," she stabbed at an olive in her salad. It rolled away. "You won't have anyone here to cook for you."

"I can eat at a restaurant or hire a cook. I can't buy grandchildren."

"And I can't buy a groom." She finally

speared the olive. "Besides, Justin and Gabe are older. Look to them for your first grand-children."

Her father snorted. "Those boys gotta be roped into pretending to play married for your fashion shows. No way they're gonna tromp down the aisle for a long time yet. You — well, a woman's got to pay mind to her clock."

Just then, the grandfather clock in the living room chimed.

"*That* is the only clock I'm minding."

Daddy could have given lessons to a pit bull. Once he got hold of something, he wouldn't let go. He knocked his knuckles on the table. "Boys, you need to help your sister."

"We are, Dad. You're making us do that show for her."

"Yeah, well, it's high time you dug up a nice young man to ask her out."

"Actually, we do know this one guy. . . ."

The way Gabe perked up made Della's blood run cold. "And you know me even better. If you dare try to pair me up with someone, I'll return the favor and double it."

Daddy slapped the table. "Good! You know someone for each of your brothers?"

Della pasted on the smile she knew gave

her brothers the willies. "Oh, I know a couple of girls for each of them, Daddy. I'd want them to have a choice, you know." She turned to her father. "In fact, a bride came in the other day with her mother. Her mama's a widow, Daddy — just perfect for you. I —"

"You're at the table," he groused. "You should eat and not talk so much."

THREE

"Okay. You've got the stance right. Now choke up on the bat a little more."

Della wrestled with the bat as she listened to Vanessa's instructions. Vanessa managed to drag her to church about three times a year, and the second time Della attended, she'd seen the announcement in the bulletin that they wanted more players on the softball team. "I'm on the team. You could join up," Vanessa urged.

"I'm not going to become a member of a church just to play ball."

"You don't have to. No strings attached."

Della confessed, "I'm miserable at sports. I've never hit a ball. They won't want me."

Vanessa proved her wrong. For two years now, Della suited up in a hideous orange and white baseball uniform and consistently played worse than anyone else in the whole league. Still, everyone wanted her to come back for more. She loved it.

29

But she'd only connected with the ball once. Kip called it the law of averages — sooner or later, it had to happen by mistake. He pretended to do the math and announced she ought to connect once every three seasons. From the looks of it, he was probably right, too.

"Della." Vanessa giggled. "I said choke up on the bat — don't strangle the poor thing! What did it ever do to you?"

She loosened her grip. "How's this?"

"Much better. Now keep your eye on the ball." Vanessa pitched, and the ball came whizzing past. "That was in the strike zone. You were supposed to swing."

"Give me another one."

Vanessa nodded, pulled another neon pink tennis ball from the pail, and pitched.

"Aaand she swings and misses!" Jeff sang out from behind her. "Mom, can we get them now?"

Della looked at Vanessa's nine-year-old stepson and waggled the end of the bat at him and the sleek black lab that pranced at his side. "You hang on a second. I have three more to miss before you and Lick gather them."

"Okay, but hurry. He's been waiting a long time."

"It's a good obedience exercise," Vanessa

30

called back. "Get ready, Della. One, two, three . . ."

She swung the bat.

"One more to go," Jeff told his dog.

"One more?"

Della turned as she heard Vanessa's husband's voice. "Nathan, are you making fun —" her voice died out. He wasn't alone. Walking alongside him was the gray-eyed hunk who bought the gloves at the shop yesterday.

"She still hasn't hit another one, Dad."

Della wanted to crawl in a hole and die of embarrassment.

Nathan rumpled Jeff 's hair. "Someday, she will. Della, this is Brandon Stevens. Brandon, Della Valentine."

"Ma'am." Brandon nodded.

"She's not a ma'am; she's a miss." Jeff let out a boyish bark of laughter. "And she misses the ball every time!"

"Having trouble?" Mr. Make-your-heart-go-pitty-pat asked.

"Well . . ." Della knew she had to be as pink as could be.

"Here." He slipped behind her, wrapped his long, long arms around and molded his callused hands over hers. "What's your thumb doing up here?"

31

"That's how my brothers hold their golf clubs."

"Different sport, different grip." To his credit, he didn't laugh. Instead, he eased her thumb around the bat. "Here. Good. Now lift your left elbow."

She followed his instructions.

"You're gonna smack this one halfway across the park." Confidence rang in his voice. "Okay, Vanessa, let her rip."

Vanessa picked up the last ball. "Here goes nothing."

Thwop. The pink tennis ball arced through the air and sailed toward a vacant picnic table. Della stood frozen in place as she watched it.

"That was a beaut. Do it again."

"It was the last ball," Vanessa called. "Jeff, give Lick his command."

Jeff gleefully shouted, "Fetch!"

While they gathered up two-dozen balls, the guy behind Della didn't release her. "Practice your swing. Keep your grip. Yeah. That's it. Now the elbow . . ." He led her through a couple of swings, then let go and waved his arm in an arc. "Practice makes perfect."

She chewed on her lower lip, struck her stance, and copied the moves a few times.

"Good. Now make sure you follow

32

through. When you stop the swing partway because you connect, you lose all the power."

Della laughed. "As if I'll actually connect."

His face darkened. "With that attitude, you won't."

"Della, think like the Little Red Engine," Jeff said as he handed his mother the bucket of tennis balls. "I think I can; I think I can."

"Not good enough," Brandon said curtly. "I know I can. I know I can."

Vanessa smiled. "Brandon was a SEAL, Della. Watch out, or he'll have you doing push ups, too."

"I'm good at those," she said.

The corner of Brandon's mouth twitched. "Girls' push ups?"

"No, standard. I'm not half bad at chin ups and pull ups, either."

"So if you can do those things, you have the upper body strength to swing a bat. It's just a matter of hand-eye coordination and practice."

"Yeah, well, once you get her batting up to snuff, you can teach her how to run." Nathan chuckled.

"Oh, you don't, do you?" Brandon gave Della a pained look.

"Don't what?"

"Run like a girl."

"News flash. I am a girl!"

"A girly girl," Vanessa called out merrily. "Here you go, Della. Slug this one out of the park and show them you have it in you."

"Here goes nothing," Della muttered as she took her stance.

"And there went nothin'," Jeff said from behind her a few seconds later.

"But your form was good. Tell you what: Tie a tennis ball on a length of twine in your garage. When you have a few minutes, bat at it. It'll take care of your hand-eye coordination. By next week, you'll connect."

"I wish the back room at the store were bigger. I spend most of my time there."

"In the back room?"

She laughed. "At the store. Maybe I could hang the ball from — no, I'd hit the wall with the bat."

"Hey you guys," someone hollered at them from the baseball diamond. "Are we gonna play ball, or are you planning to stand there and yak all night?"

Nathan picked up the bucket of tennis balls and wrapped his arm around Van's waist. "We're coming."

Della watched their casual affection and smiled. Jeff and Lick dashed up to join them.

"Looks like a commercial for domestic

bliss," Brandon said from beside her.

"If it's for sale, just tell me where and how much."

Brandon crooked a brow. "You don't know?" He took the bat from her and propped it over his shoulder. "You're ideally set up for reconnaissance and information gathering."

Della burst out laughing. "It's love, not warfare."

"Hey, all's fair in love and war, so the tools of the trade apply in both instances. Never waste an opportunity."

Della scooped her mitt from the grass. "It's too late by the time they reach me. The battle is fought, and they're ready to sign the peace treaty."

Brandon chuckled. "I wouldn't have guessed you'd think in those terms. You sound more like a warrior than a wedding planner."

She tossed the mitt into the air and caught it. "The secret lies in knowing when to put on the gloves and when to take them off."

"Hey." Brandon slid one leg over the bench and straddled it in the dugout. "Great strategy."

"Strategy?" Della wrinkled her cute little nose as a blush stole over her cheeks. "That wasn't strategy; it was shock."

She'd been up to bat when he was on second base. He'd seen her strike twice. The third time, she bunted — not intentionally, but because the ball was inside and didn't warrant a swing. Stunned, she stood there and watched it roll toward the pitcher as Brandon sped toward third.

"Aw, c'mon, Della. Stop being so modest. You bunted and sacrificed yourself so I'd be set up for to make a run for home."

"If only that were true. I can't take credit. I just froze."

"You've got a lot to learn," Brandon agreed. *And I wouldn't mind coaching you.* The thought slipped into his mind, and it felt right. Brandon lived by his hunches. They'd saved his life on more than one occasion. "Why don't we meet and I'll —"

"Whip me into shape?"

He winked. "Your shape is just fine, ma'am. It's your talent that needs refining."

Easy laughter bubbled out of her. "I'll have to remember that line. My brothers would love it!"

"Just how many brothers do you have?"

"Two."

He squinted. "And you didn't learn how to bat?"

"Only her lashes." Vanessa yanked her

36

ponytail through her cap. "Della's dad and brothers got caught in a time warp. They think a woman should be home, serving up food on a plate, not out running across home plate."

"They all love me," Della tacked on.

Her loyalty to her family counted for a lot in Brandon's book. He gave her an assessing look. "Love made them protect you."

She nodded.

"As if baseball is dangerous," Vanessa scoffed.

"My brother broke his leg sliding into home."

Twice, a member of his SEAL team broke a leg when they were out on a mission. Ugly, painful injuries. From the way her face paled, he figured she'd seen her brother suffer his injury. Brandon resisted the urge to smooth back a few of her errant curls. She'd been babied a lot. Judging by her presence here, she wanted to venture ahead. Anyone who had guts enough to try something deserved a chance in his book. "He's over it and running around now, right?"

Her face brightened. "Nothing slows him down."

Crack! Brandon automatically turned at the sound and whistled in appreciation as Kip hit a homer.

"Wow, I want to do that someday."

He smiled at Della. Never one to miss a golden opportunity, Brandon plowed right into the opening. "Fine. I'll take you to the batting cages. When are you free this week?"

Her pupils dilated — whether with pleasure or surprise, he couldn't say.

"Her shop is closed on Sundays and Mondays," Vanessa volunteered. She gave Della's leg a playful pat. "Go for it. Do it for the team."

Della looked up at him with her dark, shiny eyes and took his measure.

She's cautious. Smart, too. What's stronger — her loyalty to the team or her reticence?

A slow smile tilted her mouth. "For the team."

Della locked the door, turned over the CLOSED sign, and dashed to the back room. Brandon would be here in ten minutes, and she couldn't very well go to the batting cage in a silk dress. Hastily changing into neatly pressed brown slacks and a cotton blouse the color of peach sorbet, she tried to decide what to do with her hair. *Tying it back would be smart, but I look like I'm twelve when I do that.*

She twisted her foot into an athletic shoe and reached for the other when someone rattled the back door with a single, solid thump of a knock. *It's him!* She snatched the left shoe then groaned at the sight of the knotted lace.

"Hey! You okay in there?"

"Yes." She giggled as she hobbled toward the steel door. Out of habit, she still looked through the peephole. Even distorted by the fisheye lens, Brandon looked too good to be true in a dark blue T-shirt and jeans.

As if he knew she was spying on him, he ducked down a little closer and gave an exaggerated wink. "The password's 'Team'," he said in a grave tone, but his smile could have melted the door.

"The team," she opened the door, "is suffering a delay due to —"

"— an equipment malfunction," he finished as he swiped the shoe from her hand. "I'll see to it. You go ahead and change."

She looked down at her outfit and confessed, "I already did."

"Don't you have real clothes? Jeans? Shorts?"

"My jeans were in the hamper."

He nodded somberly. "Gotcha. On your last outfit before you do laundry."

Della didn't disabuse him of his faulty assumption. Instead she turned. "I'll go grab a rubber band from the register so I can tie back my hair."

"Good thinking."

When she returned, he hunkered down, wrapped his callused hand around her ankle, and twisted the shoe onto her stock-inged foot. "I gave up on trying to unknot it."

"Then what —" She looked down. "Oh." A small knot lay on the floor beside him. He'd cut it from the lace, connected the pieces, and now tugged on the ends as he finished tying it into a lopsided bow. "Thank you."

He plucked the knot from the floor and rose. "Nothing to it. Let's go."

She set the alarm and slipped out the back door. He shut it then nodded. "Good set up. Secure."

Della hitched her purse onto her shoulder. "It ought to be. My dad and brothers put it in — they're electricians."

Brandon shot her a quick look. "What company?"

"Power."

"Power?" he echoed. "Gabe and Justin are your brothers?"

"You know them?" She caught herself. "Of course you do, if you know their names."

"I've worked with them a couple of times

40

on a site." He scrutinized her features. "But your last name is Valentine. I didn't mentally place you with them."

"Oh, they're Valentines, too." She slipped her keys into the pocket of her purse. "Daddy said no one would trust 'Valentine Electric,' so he named the company 'Power.' "

He took a few long strides and opened the passenger door of a jeep. As she climbed in, he murmured, "You don't look anything like your brothers."

"They've each had a broken nose."

"Yeah," he drawled as he shut the door. As he walked around to the driver's side, he muttered under his breath, "They did it fighting back the men who wanted you."

Zing! Della shivered at the thrill of knowing the attraction wasn't one-sided. She pretended she hadn't overheard him and asked as he drove toward the edge of town, "So you work with Nathan's firm?"

He nodded.

She liked that curt, masculine mannerism. Growing up in a household of men, the abbreviated conversation, the brisk actions, and brusque ways didn't bother her. She found them oddly reassuring. If a woman wanted information from a man, she needed to prod each tidbit out of him. Della settled

41

into her seat and started in.

"So you're a former SEAL?"

"Six years." He drummed his fingers on the steering wheel. "You didn't interrogate Vanessa about me?"

"Oh, I tried," she confessed merrily. "But she just got a whole shipment of puppies; Jeff 's on summer break and 'helping' her at the shop, and I've spent hours on the phone trying to track down a certain pattern of Belgian lace for a client. The only time we actually connected on the phone, Van told me she's not a gossip and you're a good man."

"I knew I liked her."

"So the ball's in your court."

"You can't bat, but you use sports metaphors?"

"I'm all talk and no action." Once the words popped out of her mouth, Della groaned.

Deep, male laughter rippled in the air.

"See? You need to talk so I can keep my mouth shut."

"Crying for mercy, huh?"

She gave him a wry look. "You'd better believe it."

"Okay. Yeah, I was a SEAL for six years. Now I'm doing construction."

"Why did you leave the SEALs?"

His features tightened. "Got banged up." Just as quickly, he flashed her a cocky grin. "So for the sake of the team, I bugged out."

"Ah, yes, the all-important team," she nodded sagely. "What kind of injury, and how did you do it?"

"Shoulder. Training exercise."

Della dipped her head and studied a chip in her manicure.

Almost a mile later, the silence in the jeep nearly crackled. "Anything else?"

"It's not worth asking. I won't trust what you say."

"Why not?" He veered to the curb and gave her a disgruntled look.

"Because you just lied to me."

FOUR

"What gave you that notion?"

Features strained, she hitched her right shoulder. "I can tell. Listen, it's none of my business and —"

"Hang on a minute." She looked ready to open the door and bolt, so he curled his hand around her forearm. "Sorry. I'm used to dealing with people who know the rules."

"What rules? I thought you guys were all about honor and duty and integrity."

"We are. But that involves silence." He rubbed his thumb against the soft fabric of her sleeve. "No matter how or where a man's hurt, it's always a 'training exercise,' Della. The phrase is a shield for security purposes, and everyone accepts the need for that discretion."

Her brow puckered, but she didn't look up at him.

"I've been places and done things I can't discuss — not now, not ever. Flat out, that's

44

just how it is."

"Like it or lump it?" She finally looked at him. Dozens of questions glittered in her eyes, ones he'd never address. National security relied on it, but even if he were allowed to say anything, he wouldn't. Not to her.

Just like the peachy-colored material beneath his fingers, this woman was soft. There was a fineness, a femininity, about her that brought out all of his protective instincts. Part of serving his country revolved around preserving the beauty and innocence of people like her who'd be destroyed by the ugly currents beneath the international scene. A warrior paid the price by keeping silent. He'd seen plenty of teammates' relationships tear apart under the stress that silence imposed. If Della couldn't innately trust him, he might as well find it out now.

"So," he looked at her and quietly asked, "you gonna like it, or do I turn around and take you back to your shop?"

"You don't believe in compromise?"

"There's plenty of give-and-take in relationships, but some things are non-negotiable. I don't compromise my values."

Finally, she smiled. "Vanessa was right. You're a good man, Brandon Stevens. Are

45

you a good teacher?"

"Let's find out."

Thwop.

"Run!"

Brandon's bellow set Della in motion. She sped toward first base. The first baseman laughed so hard, he dropped the ball as she approached.

"Tag the base!" Brandon hollered.

She stepped on it and turned to give him a triumphant smile.

He punched the air, let out a victory yell then cupped his hands to his mouth. "You can let go of the bat now."

She looked down at the bat. Giggles of embarrassment shivered out of her. Even so, nothing took away the thrill of her achievement. He'd taken her to the batting cages three times now. She twirled the bat like a baton and called out, "It looks like the third time was the charm!"

He'd jogged out of the dugout. "There's no such thing as luck. Practice pays off."

"Be careful of your shoulder." She let him take the bat.

"Stop fussing and pay attention." The sparkle in his eyes took away the sting of his words. "We're behind. You need to earn us a run."

"Hey!" the pitcher yelled. "Is this a social or a softball game?"

Della propped a hand on her hip and called back, "Is there a third option?"

"You bet." Brandon gave her a stern look. "Winning. Never settle for anything but your goal."

The first baseman punched his fist into his glove and grinned. "That's my kinda thinking, and we're about to beat the socks off you."

Brandon let out a derisive snort and walked off to the batter's box. With a solid hit, Kip ended up on first and sent Della to second. She stood on second base and watched Brandon take his place at bat. Other guys would scuff their feet in dirt, restlessly find a stance, change their grip on the bat and take practice swings, or look around the diamond. Brandon didn't. Exuding confidence, he stepped up, assumed his stance, and watched the first ball without moving an inch.

"Outside. Ball one."

A moment later, the ball went whizzing by. Della let out a whoop and headed for third.

"Run, Della!" Vanessa and her twin, Valene, shouted in unison. When she hit third, Vanessa waved.

Della waved back.

"Go home!" Vanessa screamed.

"I can't believe it," Kip said later as the whole team wolfed down barbequed hot dogs. "You didn't just hit the ball. You made it on base and got a run!"

She beamed up at Brandon. "I owe it all to my coach."

Brandon swiped the mustard from her. "Next, I'll teach you how to run."

"Told you she runs like a girl." Nathan tore open a bag of chips and passed them down the picnic table. "That's going to be a real challenge."

"Me being a girl, or me running like one?"

"No complaints about what you are, ma'am." The left corner of Brandon's mouth kicked up in a rascal's grin. "In fact, it might come in handy. Are you doing anything on Saturday, the fifth?"

She thought for a moment. "Yes."

"Change your plans, and go with me to my cousin Linda's wedding."

Della shook her head rapidly and blinked as if she couldn't quite process what he'd asked. "Only a man could blend running and a wedding in the same breath."

"Self-preservation." Kip slapped Brandon on the shoulder. "Makes perfect sense to me."

"Careful!" Della half rose. "Brandon — your shoulder! Is it —"

"I'm fine." He didn't look fine at all. Deep grooves bracketed the corners of his mouth.

Della's instinct was to fuss over him, but she quelled the urge. He had that macho, I-can-take-it look. Instead, she covered for him. "So that pained look is because you're thinking about having to wear a suit for the wedding?"

"Yup." Gratitude flashed in his eyes. "I'm going to swelter."

"Guess again." She took a long, lazy lick of her Chocolate Decadence ice cream and gave him a jaunty grin. "Now that you mentioned it's Linda's wedding, I remember all of the details. I planned the whole affair with her. It's an outdoor event, and they're doing a picnic-style reception. The invitations came with a map to Seaside Park and mentioned casual wear."

"Yes!" He made a fist and jerked it downward in a pumping action — the same one her brothers used whenever they were particularly pleased with something.

Come to think of it, Brandon managed to find joy in the simplest of things. It was a good quality. Admirable. Then again, she had yet to learn something about him that she didn't like. But it would have been far more thrilling if he'd been that excited about her going to the wedding with him.

"Were you already going?" Vanessa asked her.

"Most of Granite Cliffs is." Della smiled. "It's why they're holding it outside — so there'll be enough room."

"But you're going with me," Brandon asserted.

It sounded more like an order than a question to her, but Della smiled. She didn't mind a nice guy like Brandon getting a tiny bit possessive of her. She found it flattering.

That thought crossed her mind later that evening. She'd never liked the guys around her acting domineering. In fact, she'd quickly parted company with more than one guy because he'd been too controlling. The fact that her brothers made pests of themselves actually came in handy on those occasions.

But Brandon didn't behave like a caveman who wanted to boss her around. He treated her as though she had a brain and was able to think for herself. Never once had he said she couldn't do something — he'd taken the time to teach her how to bat, promised he'd teach her to change the oil in her car, and yet never failed to be a gentleman by opening doors for her or

50

showing small courtesies.

This guy is too good to be true.

So far, they'd met at her shop or in the park. Daddy, Justin, and Gabe didn't have a clue that she'd been seeing Brandon. The first two times Brandon picked her up at work, it had been simple expediency — the last time was because she still wanted a chance to decide if things stood enough of a chance for her to endure the third-degree grilling from her family if her relationship with Brandon continued.

Pulling back her white eyelet duvet and sliding between pale pink sheets, Della wondered how The Meeting would go. When she'd seen the case of oil in Brandon's jeep, he'd offered to change her oil today, too. She'd gotten bold and told him she'd rather learn to do it herself. Tomorrow ought to be interesting.

Daddy wouldn't wait for Brandon to knock on the door — he'd stand on the porch so he could do what he termed, "Taking the man's measure." Over the years, Della learned that involved a complex combination of noticing not only what vehicle her date drove, but whether it was freshly washed, the engine sounded smooth, what any bumper stickers might say, how the man walked, dressed, and about two hundred other silly things.

For the first time, she had a feeling the man walking up to the porch would meet Daddy's requirements. Then again, Brandon had made such a stunning first impression on her, she wasn't exactly impartial. But her subsequent impressions were even more favorable.

Brandon Stevens just kept getting better and better.

FIVE

Brandon didn't bother to hide his grin. She said she wanted to learn how to do things for herself, and changing the oil in her car ought to have been a simple, straightforward exercise. Only with her, nothing ever was.

She'd insisted on learning the names of the components of the engine and sing-songed them under her breath to recall their names. Dainty little Della had a voice that would detonate grenades.

She drew out the oil stick with more flourish than a swashbuckling pirate and tried to discuss the varying colors of clean-to-dirty oil with the intensity of an artist mixing a paint palette for a masterpiece. She thought maybe she ought to shake or stir the oil before adding it. Left to her own devices, the woman could destroy an entire motor-cade in an hour.

"What?" Della shifted from one foot to the other and scrunched her nose.

"You're cute."

"I'm capable. That's more important. See? I knew if someone showed me, I could learn this."

He nodded gravely. "Just one more thing . . ."

"I thought you said that was all it took. Did I forget something?"

Brandon swiped a rag from the workbench and rubbed a streak of oil from her forehead. "Next time, don't rub your face when you've got goop on your hands."

"I've got oil on me?"

The glee in her voice made him laugh. "Yes." He dabbed at the bridge of her nose. "Hey. You've got freckles!"

She looked mortified at that discovery then quickly reached up and rubbed her finger across the spot he'd just bared, leaving another smudge. "I don't know what you're talking about."

Brandon propped a hip against the car and gave her an amused look. "Della, freckles are —"

"Don't say it!"

"What's wrong with looking —"

Her glower dared him to finish his sentence. He wasn't a man to back down from a dare. "Spicy."

Her eyes widened in shock.

"What?" he taunted. "You expected me to say something cliché like cute?"

"I should have known better. You're not like everyone else."

"Nope, I'm not." He leaned toward her. "And I'm not about to miss out on seeing all of the cinnamon and spice on your cheeks."

To his delight, she stood still as he wiped off the streak of oil she'd used to cover her freckles. He didn't stop at just that smudge, but flipped the cloth to a clean spot and continued to buff the makeup off her cheekbones. "Why do you wear all of this stuff?"

"Because I don't want to be cute. I want people to take me seriously."

"Sweetheart, you'll always be beautiful. It's not how you look that matters; it's how you act."

"Oh, great. I'm sunk." As soon as she spoke, she groaned. "See? I talk before I think. Daddy says I need to wear heels just so I can't run everywhere I go."

"I've seen you run. Heels wouldn't make any difference."

"What's wrong with how I run?"

"Everything," he said succinctly.

"Huh-unh! It gets me where I want to go!"

The memory of seeing her run around the bases caused him to let out a bark of laughter. "Della, your running does get you there, but the idea of running is to go directly to your destination."

"I just said I get there."

He strove to come up with a way to explain the problem. "Yes," he drawled, "You do get there, but you manage to go up and down and side-to-side as much as you go forward."

"Are you saying," she asked in an arctic tone, "I wiggle?" When he nodded, her chin raised a notch. "Impossible."

"Hey — you're the one who pointed out you're a woman."

"A lady. And ladies glide; they do not wiggle or bounce."

"Who fed you that line?"

"Miss M—" Her brows arched. "What does it matter?"

Everything about you matters. He didn't dare tell her that. Instead he slammed down the hood of her car and shook his head. "I can't figure you out."

"That makes two of us!"

"You can't figure yourself out, or you can't figure me out?"

"Both!"

"Babe, I'm easy. What you see is what you get."

"Well, it's the same for me."

"No, it's not. Underneath that makeup and behind whatever lessons Miss Someone-or-Other taught you, there's a real woman."

"For your information, I am a real woman, and I can cover my freckles if I want to." She yanked at the hem of her strawberry-colored T-shirt, leaving oily streaks on it. "And you have no right to pass judgment on Miss Mannerly. She was a wonderful woman, and —" She huffed. "Oh, forget it. I don't have to explain myself to you."

As she turned to stalk off, Brandon grabbed her arm. "Hang on."

"Are you okay, princess?" her father called from the porch.

"Of course I am, Daddy. Just a little greasy."

Her father hustled down the steps with a roll of paper towels. "I saw that. Don't know why you're doing this. Your brothers and I can change the oil for you."

"A little oil never hurt anyone," Della placated as she accepted a paper towel and wiped off her hands. "You never fuss when it's olive oil."

"That's different," her father scoffed.

Brandon leaned against the car again. "How is it different?"

"It ruins everything."

"Like what?"

Her father seemed almost nonplussed by the simple question. He finally stammered, "The balance. Yes." He nodded as if he'd solved the complex question entirely. "It ruins the balance."

"What balance?" Della gave her father a quizzical look.

"Princess, you already do so much for the men in your life. You need to let us do things like this to make up for it."

"Since when," she asked her father in an exasperated tone, "did we keep accounts of who does what for whom?"

Brandon held up his hand. "Hang on. I didn't mean to cause a problem. It just occurs to me, Della needs some basic skills so if her car ever goes on the fritz, she isn't stranded."

"I gave her a membership in the Auto Club," her father shot back. "My daughter is demure, and it's insane for a girl to have to do these things." He looked at her. "Your brothers and I made a vow."

"Oh, not that again," she moaned.

"What kind of vow?" Brandon sensed he'd finally stumbled across something that would explain aspects of Della that puzzled him.

"She's a girl."

"This isn't important," Della cut in hurriedly. "Daddy, we need to clean up here. I —"

"Oh, we have a few minutes," Brandon drawled.

"Her brothers and I promised each other we weren't going to rear her to be a tomboy. She deserved to grow up to be a lady, and we've done everything we could to make sure she did."

"You've done a good job. Della's a fine young woman." Brandon lifted her hand and squeezed it, leaving a smudge. "But a little grit or grease won't ever change what's on the inside."

"Doesn't change the fact that we can do stuff for her."

"As much as Della loves you, I'd bet she'd rather have you do things with her instead of for her."

"You're changing the balance," her father muttered.

Brandon let out a chortle. They both looked as if he'd taken leave of his senses. "Fair's fair. Ever since I met Della, I've been off balance."

Brandon squinted through the dust and evaluated the effect of having knocked down the wall. "Looks good, guys. Let's do the

59

other side, too."

Work boots crunched through fallen plaster as the men followed his instructions and demolished the second wall. Nathan hadn't been kidding when he said Brandon would be working with a skeleton crew. Then again, Brandon liked it that way. This project relied on detail, and his small crew took pride in the restoration.

As it turned out, the western exposure of the downstairs featured two walls that weren't shown in the original blueprints and bore no weight. Tearing down those walls was a no-brainer. Brandon watched the dust settle and knew a sense of satisfaction that this place would be functional, yet very true to the original design.

A little strip of old wallpaper appeared where it had been protected beneath one of the walls. Taking out his pocketknife, he painstakingly peeled a long swatch. With all of the choices available, he'd like to have the decorator find something that matched as closely as possible.

The hardwood floors upstairs were all in decent shape, but the downstairs ones were beyond redemption. Well — almost. He'd marked boards around the edges of the rooms that he deemed salvageable. Those were pried up, taken upstairs, and left in a room designated as a storage place for all hardware, boards, and trims they could reuse.

Brandon looked at the site with pride. It was coming along beautifully, and he loved coming to work each day to get more done. He grabbed a push broom and started cleaning up the mess as his team carted out the beams and plaster. A quick glance outside let him know the day was about over, and he wanted this place shipshape. Jim Martinez was coming over to show samples for restoration work. Better, though, when he'd mentioned it to Della, she'd invited herself along so she could see how the renovation was going.

Until now, he wouldn't allow anyone near the site who didn't have a job to do. It was just plain dangerous. With Della, it would have been downright insane. He'd found a daredevil streak in her that alternately pleased and appalled him. Visions of her twisting her ankle or falling kept him up part of the night, so he'd called this morning and told her she couldn't step foot on the place if that dainty little size five-and-a-half was in a heel.

Jim arrived with an armful of catalogs and went back out to his truck to bring in samples of hardware and moldings. Brandon gave the place a quick inspection then went out to offer to help carry things in. The minute he saw Della talking to Jim, jealousy flashed through him.

He and Della didn't have an agreement to date each other exclusively, but that didn't matter. No one else was getting a chance. Della managed to befriend everyone she met — the new checker at the grocery store, the county parking meter inspector — no one crossed her path without the woman cheerily making them feel as if they were the most important person in the universe. She had no idea how alluring that was to a man, and Brandon marveled she didn't have a ring on her finger and a slew of kids by now. One thing for certain: He wasn't going to step aside and let anyone else have a chance at her. She was his.

"I'll make a reservation," Jim said to her as Brandon jogged up.

"Perfect!"

He stopped dead in his tracks. She wanted to date Jim?

Six

"Brandon!" She turned her thousand-watt smile on him.

"You two know each other?" The question grated out of him.

"We sure do." Della stepped to Brandon's side and brushed plaster dust from his sleeve.

A glint flashed in Jim's eyes, and he shook his head. "Not that it means much. Granite Cliffs is so small, everyone knows everyone else."

Still not mollified, Brandon asked, "So what kind of reservations are you making?"

"Supper." Jim hefted a case from his truck. "Della found out where Katie's dad proposed to her mom."

Realizing he'd reacted to a non-existent threat, Brandon relaxed and tucked Della into his side and jerked the case of hardware samples away from Jim. "Obviously Granite Cliffs is bigger than you think, because I've never met anyone named Katie."

"She's been in Europe for the past six weeks." Jim pulled out another case, and they started toward the house. "Gawking at cathedrals and famous buildings."

Della slipped her arm around Brandon's waist and squeezed. "Katie's in college — an architecture major."

"And absence made Jim's heart grow fonder." Brandon steered her around a clump of azaleas he'd specifically guarded during the renovation.

Della entered the huge, old building and slipped from his hold. She slowly spun around, surveying the place. "Oh, this is magnificent!"

"Yeah," Brandon agreed, but her reaction pleased him to no end. "But it needs a bunch of work still."

She tugged on the case he held. "What are we waiting for? This place is perfect for wedding receptions!"

Jim chuckled. "There's no hurry, Della. Knowing Katie, she'll want a long enough engagement to plan everything down to the last detail."

Slowly rubbing his thumb back and forth while he continued to cup Della's shoulder, Brandon asked, "So if it were yours, sweetheart, what would you do?"

■ ■ ■ ■

"I must be out of my mind." Della crammed her hands into the pockets of her windbreaker. She'd been in such a great mood last evening, deciding on moldings and trims and a kitchen layout for the place Brandon was remodeling, he'd somehow managed to get her to agree to a morning jog. "I can't believe I'm up this early."

"Sissy." Brandon yanked her away from his jeep and toward the edge of the parking lot. "You said you didn't want anyone watching. This is perfect timing. Tide's going out. The sand at the tide line is hard packed, and we own the beach."

She didn't argue. He'd been good enough to honor her request for someplace that wasn't crowded. With anyone else, she'd feel vulnerable out here, all alone. Brandon could protect her against anything.

He wore a ratty T-shirt with an almost-washed-to-death US Navy emblem on the front and a pair of gym shorts he should have pitched into the ragbag years ago. Impervious to the tendrils of morning fog drifting in the chilly air, he plowed ahead.

"I must be crazy," she muttered under her breath. *Love makes you do foolish things.*

The thought made her stumble in a small pile of sand that had drifted onto the asphalt.

Brandon caught her, held her steady. "You okay?"

I'm falling in love with you. Afraid he'd see the truth in her eyes, she ducked her head and rested against him, listening to the steady beat of his heart. "*Mmm.* You're warm."

He didn't seem in a hurry to let go of her. For a few minutes, he held her close then briskly chafed his hands up and down her arms. "There. Let's get busy." He started doing some stretches, and she copied him. "Warm up. No muscle pulls on my watch."

"Aye, aye, sir."

"Feeling sassy, are you?"

"No, I'm still too cold to waste my breath arguing."

"You'll be warm soon enough."

Once they finished warming up, they hiked through the sand to the water's edge. Brandon stopped, rested his hands on his hips, and instructed, "Now run."

"With you watching?"

"Ten yards. Do it."

Self-conscious as could be, she did as he bade. When she turned around, he'd squatted near her footprints. "What are you do-ing?"

"Come look." He waited until she joined him then pointed at the imprint her athletic shoes left behind. "Your heel imprint is the deepest, the ball of your foot leaves a perfect impression, and then your toe digs in."

"What does that mean?"

"You land wrong and don't push off. You lose your impetus by bouncing up instead of pushing off. When you have that impetus, you'll lengthen your stride, too."

"Oh." What else could she say? It made sense, but she didn't know exactly how to correct the problem. "I always thought run-ning is just fast walking."

He shook his head. "No wonder you run like a woman. Listen up: Impact on the very back of your heel will hurt you." One of his hands curled around her ankle as the other cupped the top of her foot. "Put your hand on my shoulder."

She took care to use his left shoulder. Warmth and strength radiated from him.

He jostled her ankle. "Let loose. Relax."

"Oh. Okay." She forced herself to pay at-tention.

"You want to basically hit almost flat-footed and use your ankle to push off." His hands guided her foot as he gave the instruction. He did it a few times.

"So it's sort of like walking in heels, but not."

He looked up at her, eyes full of mirth. "I wouldn't know."

She laughed. "I land the same, but I don't toe off. If I pushed off with my ankle in heels, I'd walk right out of them."

Brandon chuckled, rose, and dusted off his hands. "Hold my hand."

She clasped his right hand with her left. "Now what?"

He briskly rubbed her hand. "I'll bring gloves for you next time."

"I'm starting to warm up a little."

"Good. Now start running around me. Begin with your normal form, and when you've hit your stride, I'm going to pull you faster. That'll give you forward impetus so you can feel the difference when you push with your ankles instead of toes."

"Good thing I don't get dizzy easily." She started jogging, and he rotated about like a hub as she wheeled round him.

"Pick it up." His grip tightened, and he rotated a little faster, then faster still. "I'm going to let go. Keep your form and run along the same line you ran last time."

Once he released her, she dashed down the beach.

"Okay. Come back!"

When she turned around, his grin made getting up so early and having sand in her shoes worth it. "Well?"

"Take a look at your footprints."

She stood beside him and compared them. "My stride is longer!"

"Significantly longer. Less effort, more distance."

"The ball of my foot dug deeper, and my toes aren't digging holes."

"Yup. Now that you have the basic form, let's get a move on." He started to jog in the dry sand, and she scurried alongside him.

"Loose sand is harder. I'll move —

"Nope." He gave her an indulgent smile. "I'm used to ten-mile runs in this each morning. I don't want to get soft."

"Ten miles!"

"You're going to that lifeguard station and stopping." He gestured toward a spot about half a mile away. "Respect your limits and push a little more each day. In a few weeks, you'll be going five miles and will barely break a sweat."

"Ladies, do *not* —" she refuted then took another breath before she finished, "— sweat."

"No?"

69

"They glow."

When they reached the lifeguard station, Brandon swooped her up, swung her around, and chortled. "You're pretty when you glow."

"When I . . . catch my breath . . ."

"Don't." His head dipped, and he kissed her.

Della was sure she'd never catch her breath again.

SEVEN

Delicate, lily white. Soft. Brandon couldn't get over the feel of Della's hand in his. He'd positioned them on the bride's side of the park where Della would be able to see the ceremony, yet he'd be on the very outside edge so his height wouldn't block folks' view from farther back.

When he'd arrived to pick up Della for the wedding today, Mr. Valentine stood on the porch like a general inspecting the troops. After he'd taken his time, he shut one eye and squinted through the other, then rumbled, "Haven't run you off yet?"

Sensing plenty lay beneath the wry humor, Brandon stared him in the eye. "I'm not going anywhere."

"You're big, but if you make my baby girl cry, I'll make every last inch of you hurt, and hurt bad."

Yeah. Well, Brandon couldn't blame him. Della called forth a man's instincts to shield

71

his woman. Even now, a quick glance at her dainty, pale green sundress and strappy sandals made Brandon shift position so he'd cast Della into his shadow. She'd twisted her hair into a froth of curls at the top of her head, leaving springy little wisps at her nape. His brows knit. Fair skinned and freckled, she'd burn if he didn't keep her in the shade.

As weddings went, it was a nice one. Getting hitched when a couple was this wild about one another rated as a smart move, and Brandon liked seeing how this bride and groom were head-over-heels in love. But Brandon wished the pastor would limit the affair to simple vows and a short prayer. Instead, he inserted comments about Jesus' first miracle being at a wedding feast and other Christian stuff. Especially with it being summer and all, he could have taken mercy on the guests, who stood in the hot sun, and just gotten down to business.

As soon as the newlyweds kissed, Brandon swiped Della into the shade of a big, old sycamore. She didn't come alone; she dragged Annette with her. He would have enjoyed trying to get a kiss from Della, but having an audience squelched that notion.

"Brandon, could you bring a chair over here for Annette? A glass of water, too."

He looked at his wilting sister-in-law. She rested a hand on a just-beginning-to-bulge belly. "I'm going to pound my brother into the ground for leaving you alone in this condition."

Annette's laughter sounded a tad faint. "Don't beat him up. I need him."

"He's a good man." The curls atop Della's head danced as she nodded her head to punctuate her praise. "In fact, Dave did a great job on the music. He's never let on that he's so talented. He needs to get cards made up, and I'll recommend him to my clients."

"Really? How nice." Annette stroked her belly. "This little one is going to be expensive, and we just blew through our nest egg last year when we went on our twenty-fifth anniversary cruise."

Brandon hadn't seen a woman who could be as animated as Della, yet turn into such a gentle listener. She definitely was one-of-a-kind. He hiked off and came back with two bottles of iced water in his pockets and a pair of folding chairs. "Both of you rest and cool off."

"Oh, I thought I'd go help spread out the picnic blankets and —"

Brandon winked. "Annette needs some company. I'll go help."

"He's afraid I'll start crying again," Annette said in a stage whisper. "It's gotten to be a habit of mine lately."

"Soon, it'll be the baby crying, not you." Della twisted off the top of the water bottle and handed it to her.

Brandon opened the other and tucked it into her hand. It didn't take long to help spread out a variety of nifty plaid blankets. A caterer had the picnic theme down pretty well — barbecued ribs and hamburgers, corn on the cob, big pans of fried chicken, and vats of salads. Brandon mentally planned on plowing through and piling up plates for Della, Annette, and himself.

"Hey, Stevens."

He turned. "Gabe. Justin."

"What do you think you're doing with our sister?"

Brandon didn't sense any hostility. Appreciating how they kept watch over their sister, he pretended to study the pair and kept his tone light. "Della's a sweet little gal. How'd she ever end up with brothers like you?"

"That's not the issue." Gabe closed in. "You'd better treat her right."

"Not a problem." After having worked with the Valentine brothers, Brandon wasn't in the least bit surprised that they matched their father's bluster. Reliable, good workers, a bit high-spirited, but solid through and through. They loved Della every bit as much as she loved them — and because of that, Brandon determined to earn their respect and trust.

Justin smirked. "Dad told us to find someone to date her. I was going to nominate you, but don't tell her that." Brandon chuckled. "I won't — unless she asks. The little lady already had me promise to always shoot straight. I'm not going back on my word." He shoved a pair of blankets into Gabe's arms. "So stop swaggering and make yourselves useful. Spread these out."

Gabe stared pointedly at Brandon's empty arms. "What are you going to do?"

"I'm going back to your sister." He turned and strode toward the sycamore tree.

Annette laughed as he approached. "I told Della to stop fretting about you talking with her brothers. If they irritate you, you'll handle them."

"Yup." He winked.

"But you're too smart to irk them," Della decided. "I'm the one who'll bug you first."

"You already do." Brandon took her hand and lifted it in a silent bid for her to rise. She followed his lead beautifully in a single, fluid move, and he fought the urge to yank

75

her close as he growled, "You make me crazy."

He escorted them to the reception line, and Brandon couldn't help thinking Della would be beautiful in a bridal gown. *Standing next to me.*

While in the SEALs, he'd refused to be in a serious relationship because it was just too hard on the woman and unfair to kids. Now his life was stable. For the first time, the idea of marriage, a little house, and kids slammed into him. The impact didn't blow him away, though. Elation filled him. He'd always loved family. Maybe the time had come for it to be his turn.

And Della would make a fine wife.

"Dry? Is that you?"

Della watched in surprise as Jordan slapped Brandon on the back. Valene's husband shook his head. "I almost didn't recognize you. You clean up well."

"Dry?" Della accepted the plate someone handed her and looked at the men in puzzlement.

"We ran into each other, compliments of Uncle Sam."

Brandon's casual voice could have fooled an acquaintance, but Della detected a wealth of information and feeling under the surface.

"I never figured out," Jordan continued, "whether you got that handle because you never drank or because you were famous for snaking."

"Both."

"You ate snakes?" Annette turned a hideous shade of green.

"Nah. Snaking is just crawling through stuff you don't want to know about." As if his height didn't give him a good enough view of the huge spread of food, Brandon craned his neck and gawked ahead. "Now I wouldn't mind crawling through this stuff one bit."

Della took the hint that he didn't want to pursue the topic and rescued him. "I get dibs on the potato salad before you do. It's from Pudgy's."

Annette regained her coloring and grabbed a fork. "Okay, I give up. You two go pick up the whole bowl and bring it back to me. I'll be sitting in the shade." As she waddled off, Della started laughing.

Brandon arched a brow and warned, "She was serious."

"I know! That's what's so funny. I'm glad she's finally over her morning sickness. I'll make a plate for her and add a big scoop."

"I'll hold all three plates." He followed her down the buffet line and back toward Annette. "I'll go back for drinks."

"But Jordan just said you don't drink."

"I don't." He regretted his curt tone. "My granddad drank himself into the grave. The whole family suffered from what booze did to him."

She nodded somberly. "My mom was killed by a drunk driver. I understand."

"Sorry." He studied her. "How old were you?"

"It was just before my first birthday."

He whistled under his breath.

Della didn't want to spoil their day with a recitation of what she'd missed. She did a little hop-step to match his stride and laughed. "Yeah, I was at my dad and brothers' mercy for a long time, but I paid them back for all of their mistakes while I learned to cook."

"So you can cook?"

"Daddy taught my brothers how to do wiring by having them install smoke detectors in every room of the house. Whenever I burned anything, the whole neighborhood knew. You can bet I learned quick!"

"Her lasagna is to die for," Annette said as she reached for her plate.

"Is that so?"

Della laughed. "You're welcome to come try it, but you'll have to fight Daddy and my brothers to get any."

He gave her a slow wink that made her toes curl. "Some things are worth fighting for."

"You pulled that off beautifully," Brandon said as he drove away from the reception. "No one knew it fell in your lap as a last-minute deal, and if I hadn't seen your plans back at the shop, I wouldn't have known you plotted the set up and made all of the arrangements."

"That's the way it's supposed to seem — effortless. The spotlight is on the bride and groom."

"Yeah, well, this wasn't exactly the standard wedding and reception. Take some credit, Della. You stepped in and saved the day by putting this together. Doing the picnic theme was a stroke of genius."

"Coping with glitches is part of my business. It wasn't what Linda originally wanted, but I'm glad the outcome pleased her. I just used some creativity to get the job done. I'm sure you handle predicaments all the time, too."

"Not that kind." He changed lanes and glanced at her. "Linda turned into a basket case when the caterer bugged out."

"She looked serene today." Della twisted as far as her seat belt allowed and faced him. "Everyone pitched in to make it come together."

"The preacher got too long-winded." Brandon flipped the jeep's sun visor to the side. "He could have just stuck to the usual prayer and vows. Hot as it is, we all fried in the sun while he talked about Jesus and that stuff."

"Plugging some kind of minisermon is his trademark with all of the weddings he conducts. Pastor MacIntosh is a nice guy, but according to him, I'm doomed to hell because I'm not a Christian."

Brandon snorted. "You're a good person. If God is love and forgives, then you'll go to heaven."

"Whew!" Della shoved back strands of hair blowing about her face. "We've never talked about religion. I don't know why we have to believe in a bunch of stories in the Bible. Living right and doing good should be all that counts."

"I'm all for America, family, and clean living."

"I knew from the day we met you were a patriot and dedicated to your family. I could tell you didn't smoke because you don't smell icky. Today I found out you don't drink."

"Keeping a score card?" There was a wealth of meaning behind his question.

"That sounds calculating."

"Hey — we've never shied away from a subject yet. Why start now?" He'd begun to think in terms of a future together, and he needed some reassurance that she felt likewise. Just how serious was she about making this relationship work?

"Okay." She paused. "What do you want to know?"

Survival skills like reading body language, nuances of expressions, the slightest shift of posture or change in blink rate didn't evaporate just because he'd left the SEALs. She'd folded her hands in her lap.

"Why are you withdrawing?"

"I'm not withdrawing."

He pulled to the shoulder of the road and swept his hand through the air at her posture. "The way you're sitting screams 'Not a chance.' "

Her brown eyes grew huge as color washed her cheeks. Her lips parted, then closed, then parted once again as her chin lifted. "No, there isn't a chance."

The words hit him with the impact of a mortar shell.

EIGHT

"I just can't." She looked down then back at him. "I mean — well, I know it's nothing to lots of people. I don't feel that way, though. Call me old fashioned, but I'm waiting."

Her words sank in, and Brandon finally started breathing again. "Waiting."

She nodded jerkily. "For marriage."

"That's not where this was headed."

Wariness still radiated from her darkened eyes, and the corners of her mouth tensed. If anything, she looked worse. Brandon quickly replayed what he'd just said and wanted to kick himself. *She thinks I just said our relationship isn't headed for marriage.*

He reached over and rubbed his thumb over her whitened knuckles. "Face it, Della: After several dates, we've barely kissed. I got the picture at the very start, and it's fine. Maybe not easy" — he gave her a lopsided smile — "but good stuff rarely comes easy."

Her guard still didn't drop. Her voice sounded hoarse as she said, "I'm not just playing hard-to-get, Brandon. It's not a game."

"I understood that." He frowned. "You misunderstood me. What I'm saying is, I respect you. The first time we met, I said I didn't compromise my values; I don't ask others to ditch theirs either."

As his words sank in, she slowly slumped back into the seat like a parachute losing wind. The sweetest smile he'd ever seen erased the anxiety lines bracketing her mouth.

"You got all intense, and I figured you were . . ."

"Putting the move on you?" he supplied when her voice died out.

She nodded.

"The chemistry's all there, but that's only part of the equation." He leaned back against the door of the jeep and felt the whole vehicle rock as a truck whizzed past. "I don't know where this relationship is going to end up, but I like where it's headed so far."

"Me, too." She tilted her head to the side. "So what were you trying to find out about me?"

"Let's see . . ." He drew the words out slowly to tease her. "I already know you don't smoke. You favor one particular perfume that drives me nuts. You don't drink. You're highly intuitive and sensitive, which is probably why your shop is so successful. And your dad and brothers are over-protective."

"How did you know that?"

"Because Gabe's stalking toward us, and from the sounds of it, Justin's coming up on my blind side."

"Oh, no," she groaned.

Brandon couldn't believe what he was seeing. Then again, he should have. Wherever they went or whatever they did, one of Della's brothers or her dad usually managed to make an appearance. He raised his voice. "Justin, I'm taking your sister to the grocery store."

"Doesn't look like it." The reply sounded as if Justin was jogging closer.

"I'm going to talk her into making me some lasagna."

"No way." The brothers converged on the jeep at the same time. A greedy gleam replaced the anger on Gabe's face.

"I told you they decimate the pan," she folded her arms.

"So I'll be sure we buy a second pan along

with the fixings."

Justin leaned against the car. "Just be careful. If Della offers you garlic bread, she's trying to rope you into doing something."

"Garlic bread, huh?"

"Homemade," Gabe said succinctly.

"Didn't know it would take that much time." Brandon winked at her. "Guess I'll just take you out for supper instead, Babe. Say good-bye to your brothers."

"Bye, Justin. Bye, Gabe." Barely restrained laughter bubbled under her words. Moments after Brandon put the jeep in gear, she cleared her throat. "They're going to make you pay for this."

He caught sight of her brothers in his rear view mirror and smiled. "Some things are worth fighting for."

"Camping?" Della repeated the word as if it came from a foreign language.

"Yeah. Jim and Katie, Val and Jordan are all on board. We'll head out Saturday morning — just to the San Bernardino Mountains."

"My shop —" She looked around then huffed when his grin didn't fade one iota. "I can't just shut down for four days."

"You don't have to. You're already closed on Sundays and Mondays. Ellen Zobel can cover for you on Saturday, Tuesday, and Wednesday."

"You already spoke with Van and Val's mom?"

"Hold on." He raised his hands as if to ward her off.

"This had better be a good explanation, because I'm pretty ticked off right about now."

The rascal dared to wink at her. If she were a violent person, Della thought she might kick him in the shins just to watch that cocky smile fade. He had no call to go arrange things regarding her business.

"Nathan brought Ellen by my worksite. He said it was to let her see the house, but I think he did it so I couldn't deck him for telling me he's shutting my site down for half a week so he can swipe my men. Ellen volunteered."

She folded her arms and arched a brow. "Before or after you asked?"

"How would I have known she's filled in for you in the past? Come on, Della. We'll have fun."

"Fun."

His head dipped and rose once in a display of pure, arrogant assurance. "I'll teach you everything you need to know."

"I'll embarrass you," she warned. Secretly,

she longed to go on the trip, but she felt obliged to confess something. "I've never been camping."

"Starlight. Campfire. Fresh air . . ."

"Dirt, spiders, and wild animals . . ."

He leaned so close, his breath teased across her face as he whispered, "Hot cocoa and s'mores."

"Oh, that's not fair." She laughed. "You know I can't turn down chocolate."

"I know." He kissed her then straightened up. "I'll bet you have a few dozen things to tend to before we leave. Don't worry about gear. Just stuff a few shirts and a pair of jeans into a pillowcase."

"I have a sleeping bag."

"Fine. We're on."

"We're off!" she called to her father as she bounced down the stairs.

Brandon met her with a look of utter disbelief. "What is that?"

"My sleeping bag."

He snatched it from her, snorted in derision, and planted it on the floor in the corner.

"What's wrong with it?"

"Everything."

Della sat down on the steps and gave him a disgruntled look. "You said the same thing about how I ran."

"We fixed that. We'll fix this, too." He plucked her up and headed toward the door then stopped at the sight of a bulging suitcase.

"You are *not* 'fixing' that. I've cut it down to the absolute bare essentials."

"I've lived for a month out of a pack with less stuff than that, and my gear included a tent and sleeping bag."

"Men don't use curling irons or makeup."

"I carried camo face paint." He let out a world-weary sigh. "And you can ditch the curling iron because we're not going to have electricity."

"Nope. It's butane." She grabbed the handle and started to tow the suitcase over the threshold. "I thought of everything."

He shut the door and muttered, "You're taking everything."

After a quick stop at a surplus place where Brandon gave her a crash course on thermal ratings on sleeping bags, showed her how to judge quality of sleeping pads, and extolled the virtues of a few other doodads, they headed for the campground.

"Jim's flight was overbooked. He's getting in on a noon flight, so he and Katie will be here by supper. As soon as Val finishes her shift at the hospital, she and Jordan will come. We're going to select and establish a site."

Once they reached the mountains, Della couldn't sit still. "Look! Oh, it's beautiful here!"

"Yeah, but there's no water source."

She gave him a horrified look. "You're taking me someplace without plumbing?"

"Rustic accommodations."

After digesting that unwelcome and euphemistic explanation, Della decided to be a good sport. She pointed out other possible campsites.

"Not protected from the wind. Tents will blow over. . . . Too close to the creek, and the water's barely moving. Bugs would eat us alive after sunset."

Just about when she despaired of ever finding a place he'd find satisfactory, Della called out, "Wait! There." She pointed out the open window to her right.

Brandon steered the jeep into a clearing, scanned the area, and nodded. "See? All you needed was to know what to look for. Great choice."

He made the chores fun. A natural-born teacher, he'd show her how to do things and explain why it had to be done in that particular way. Everything from pounding tent stakes in at an angle to where to build a fire turned into an opportunity to learn and work side-by-side. Brandon didn't treat her like a fancy china doll that had to be cosseted — he treated her like a capable, thinking woman. No one had ever accepted her just as she was instead of trying to squeeze her into a mold and make her play a role. With Brandon, she felt free to be herself. He made it safe and fun to try new things.

By the time everyone else arrived, all three tents were pitched and a hearty stew bubbled on the camp stove. Jordan sat down at the picnic table and announced, "I'd like to bless the meal."

"Sure." Brandon thumped down his cup.

Della glanced around the table. She and Brandon were the only non-Christians. Katie and Jim didn't go to church much, but they'd immediately bowed their heads and chimed in on the *Amen.* Later, around the campfire, Katie taught them some songs she'd learned at high school church camp.

Curled up beside Brandon at the campfire rated as a highlight in Della's life. Warm, cherished, comfortable, she laughed as he torched another marshmallow into a charred mess. "How can you eat that? It's charcoal!"

"Think you could do any better?" He

stabbed another marshmallow on a stick and handed it to her. "Have at it."

"I'm great at this," she boasted. "Just ask Val. We used to have beachside picnics in high school. I'm not utterly helpless, you know."

"No one," Brandon said as he speared another ill-fated marshmallow, "with a brain like yours is helpless."

Valene cheered.

"What got into you?" Jordan gave Valene a baffled look.

"In high school, Van and I hung out with Della. We were known as Zany, Brainy, and Prissy. Someone finally realized Della's smart!"

"Acting like that, we'll all think you're zany." Jordan's voice held affection.

"Well, I'm sleepy." Katie yawned and rose.

Brandon sandwiched his marshmallow between two broken bits of graham cracker and gobbled it down. "Della's still not done with that marshmallow. When it's done, we'll extinguish the fire."

She didn't regret the last five minutes alone as the others turned in. Brandon brushed his temple against hers and murmured, "I was an idiot to eat marshmallows. I can't kiss you without leaving sticky junk on your face."

She turned and whispered, "I haven't eaten any yet. Hold still." She brushed a kiss along his jaw line then pulled away. "I guess we'd better put out the fire."

"Yeah." His gravelly undertone gave a completely different twist to her words.

Della hopped up, but Brandon captured her hand. "Some fires you put out. Others, you bank the embers so you can bring them to life again at a later time." He dumped what was left from the coffeepot onto the dying flames. "Go on and join Katie in your tent before I douse this, so you have some light."

She scampered into her tent and zipped it shut. Della didn't mention she had a tiny flashlight in her pocket.

NINE

"Della." Brandon stood outside her tent and hissed her name again. This time, he heard some rustling.

"Huh?"

"Come on out here." A few moments later, the tent zipper buzzed. He snickered when she held the flaps closed and barely peeked out with one eye. "We're on breakfast detail."

"It's still dark." Her whispered words carried more than a hint of accusation.

"Not for long."

She sighed. "Give me fifteen minutes."

"Three."

The zipper sounded, and the flap sealed completely again. Ten minutes later, she emerged. She'd pulled on neatly pressed tan slacks. He bet whatever shirt she had on beneath her jacket was just as impractical. The tip of her ponytail bounced along at her waist, and she'd somehow managed to slap on some makeup.

"You need to learn to tell time," he said as he tugged her along. He had to keep moving before he kissed her silly. Months ago, he'd thought his life was over. He'd left the "family" of SEALs. Suddenly, things had changed. He saw a future with Della, of them having their very own family — trips to the beach and camping. Rowdy little kids who jumped on their beds. . . . Seeing the woman he loved first thing in the morning jolted him. He'd found sheer contentment in a very disturbing package.

Their first stop was his jeep. Cracking open the first-aid kit, he searched for an alcohol swab. "No perfume up here unless you want to get eaten alive."

"Oh." She hastily swabbed off her wrists and behind each ear. She'd put in earrings. Dangly ones. Brandon grinned and wondered what she'd do if her told her — *oh, why not?* "Those earrings —"

"Aren't they pretty? I got them on sale."

"At Joe's Bait and Tackle?"

Her eyes grew huge. "What?!"

He reached over, unhooked it from her ear, and dangled it between them. "Looks like a great fishing lure to me."

She snagged it from him and popped it back into her earlobe. "You haven't had coffee yet. I forgive you." Leaning into the jeep to put the alcohol swab into his litterbag, she asked, "So what are we cooking?"

"Whatever we catch." He grabbed a pole from the jeep and shoved it into her hand.

"Fish for breakfast?"

Brandon chuckled softly. The glee in her voice made the whole trip worthwhile.

An hour later, Brandon sat on the shore and cast his line again. Della didn't have the patience it took to sit still and wait for a nibble. Soon after they'd started fishing, she'd stuck her pole into the dirt, tried unsuccessfully to dust off her seat, and wandered up and down the stream. She stayed in sight, and Brandon enjoyed watching her exploring the area with such intensity. Finally, she'd grabbed his net. "Careful," he called.

"It's only water." She nimbly made her way across several stones. "You said fish like cool, deep water. This looks like a good spot."

"You do know how to swim, don't you?"

"Only if I'm wearing arm floaties." Her laughter drifted to him.

Brandon smiled at her sass and spirit. She'd stolen his heart. Never one to hesitate when he'd decided on a course of action, he grimaced at the realization that Della would probably want a long engagement so she could plan the perfect wedding.

She skipped back to him. "Look what I got!"

He ignored the fish in her net and swept her in a circle then hugged her tight. "Nope. Look what I got."

Brandon couldn't get the camping trip out of his mind. Watching Della had been a real kick — the woman embraced life with such zest, he'd loved opening her eyes to all the little things around them. She'd actually gotten grubby, and he'd never seen a woman look more appealing than she did, sitting on a rock beside him, trying to copy how he held a blade of grass between his thumbs to make a whistle.

Coming back to work — well, at least he liked his job. If he didn't, he would have been sorely tempted to stay right up in the mountains with her. She'd invited him to come over for supper tonight — Power Electric worked on the site today, and her father volunteered that she'd stuffed the biggest roast he'd ever seen in the crock pot. The old adage about the way to a man's heart being through the stomach didn't hold true — she'd already captured him before he ate a bite of her cooking . . . but Della's great cooking sure sweetened the deal.

"Hey, Brandon! Did Della —" Gabe began.

"— rope you into the show, too?" Justin finished in a morose tone.

Brandon shoved his cell phone back into its holder and asked, "What show?"

"For her shop. She bullies us into tuxes, and we have to pretend to be besotted grooms." Justin measured a length of electrical wire from a spool and cut it.

"At least she's trying to line up safe 'brides' this time," Gabe said as he pulled more wire. "Van and Val are both married. Katie already has Jim."

"It's just a show. What's the problem?"

The wiring in Gabe's hands snarled just as badly as his voice. "The models are piranhas in white satin. They're total man-eaters. Get close, and your days are numbered."

Brandon chuckled. "Thanks for the warning. Della didn't ask, though, so I'm safe."

Just then, his cell phone rang again. "Hello? Della!"

Della's brothers started laughing like loons.

"Dreams can come true. . . ." Della lost her line for a moment as she watched Brandon

97

step on stage in his tux. *There ought to be a law against men that good-looking being let out alone. And I'll volunteer to escort this one. . . .*

The microphone let out a small squawk, jarring her out of her own fantasy and back to the bridal extravaganza. "The styles this season are classic and more tailored, accentuating the groom's masculinity, and they photograph especially well. . . ."

Just about every waking minute for the past week had revolved around the details for this show. Two hundred fifty brides and their mamas or sisters filled the room. Caterers, photographers, florists, stationers, jewelers, two lingerie stores, and two other bridal shops put on this extravaganza twice a year. Almost a quarter of her year's sales would be generated from the contacts here, and she took every opportunity to promote her shop.

One look at Brandon striding down the walkway in that tuxedo ought to make every woman in the room swoon. The rascal hit his mark at the end of the runway, half turned, and winked — at her!

"Where's the bride?" someone called out.

Della only then realized the model who was supposed to be with him hadn't materialized. She quickly extemporized, "This is the best man." *The best man I've ever seen* . . . "Next, we'll see the bride with the man of her heart. Yes, ladies, here comes the bride. . . ."

Times like this, family and friends really helped. Vanessa and Nathan, Valene and Jordan, Katie and Jim — they all radiated the contentment of couples in love. As for her brothers — for all the fuss they kicked up about getting roped into helping, they'd actually gone the extra mile and rigged up special lights and a fantastic backdrop. Two of the three models she hired as brides/bridesmaids walked the runway with flair — but one seemed to be having difficulty.

Katie tugged on the back of Della's dress and whispered from behind the curtain, "Angela's sick."

Della waited until another couple posed on the runway and hissed, "Your mom's here, isn't she?"

"Yes. Pink dress, second row."

"I hope she'll forgive me. . . ." Della smiled at the audience and looked at them. "I'd like to do something a little different today. It occurs to me that my brides are all younger women. I'd like to have a mature woman come back and show us all that love is ageless."

The idea electrified the audience. "When

love comes again, the son often has the honor of escorting his mother down the aisle. Let's have Brandon come out here to escort the 'bride' from our audience."

Brandon appeared and plucked a rose from the trellis and turned to Della.

He'd shocked her on the phone when he volunteered to help with the show before she even told him about it. Clearly, he didn't mind pitching in, and the extemporaneous action showed style.

Della stood on the toes of her already high heels. "How about if we match that rose to the dress of the woman in the audience?"

Brandon hopped off the runway with a lithe move and soon stopped in front of a pair of young, giggling girls. His voice cut through the air. "A lady in the second row since this is the second time around." He extended the rose to Katie's mother with a gallant flourish. "M'lady?"

Tessa Garrett accepted the rose and stood. "I never had a son, but I'm more than willing to adopt you!"

"There you have it!" Della said into the microphone. "An adoption and a wedding in the same afternoon."

Valene and Jordan walked the runway as Della cheerfully praised the features of their formalwear. Katie and Jim came next; then

Della glanced over and caught sight of Brandon. He stood behind the curtain, out of sight from the audience. The minute their eyes met, he held up four fingers. He didn't look apologetic or worried in the least about asking for more time. His confidence in her sent her spirits soaring.

Having done this event for the past three years, Della knew just how to organize everything backstage so the models could scurry back, change, and return. She also planned something to fill in a time lag, just in case. Taking advantage of a momentary pause, she lifted a basket. "I'm going to send this around. Slip in your cards, and at the close of the show, we'll have a drawing. Della's Bridal, Forget Me Not Flowers, and Genesis Photography have created a gift package valued at over one thousand dollars. . . ."

Minutes later, Brandon gave her a thumbs-up.

"Take a breath now, ladies, because once you see this next couple, you'll be breathless! Brandon is escorting Tessa to the altar." Brandon appeared with Tessa on his arm, and the audience burst into applause.

"Love is ageless, and so are the beautiful lines of Tessa's gown. . . ."

It barely seemed possible that she'd spent

weeks planning the show and it was over in an hour and fifteen minutes. Della mingled with prospective customers then went behind the curtains, took one look at Brandon, and burst out laughing.

TEN

"We must've done well — you're happy." Brandon grinned at her as he slowly unknotted his tie and drew it off.

"Get some orders, Sis?" Gabe asked.

"Five of the gowns are on reserve. I need to tag them." She took the tie from him. "Your feet hurt, too, Brandon?"

"I'll tag them," Vanessa offered.

"No one's toe-tagging me," Brandon protested. "I'm definitely alive and kicking."

"The gowns, not your feet." Della took the tie from him.

"No kidding," Van teased. "I've seen his feet, and I'm not that brave! Just tell me which gowns."

While Della specified which ones, Brandon tugged her over to a chair and promptly yanked off her drive-a-red-blooded-man-crazy high heels. "Why did you wear these?"

"They match my dress," she said with insane, feminine logic. "Oh, my word!

103

Brandon, what happened to your feet?" She popped out of the chair and tried to shove him from his kneeling position.

He didn't budge.

"Brandon!" Her voice took on a decided edge as she knelt beside him.

"It's nothing."

"Nothing?!" She stared at his blisters in horror.

He tilted her face up to his. "You must think I'm a real wuss if you think a couple of blisters are gonna bother me."

"Are you gonna kiss my sister?" Justin's words held unmistakable challenge.

"Your sister," Della declared as she threaded her fingers through Brandon's hair and dipped closer, "is going to kiss him."

"Over my dead body," Justin blustered.

"That can be arranged, can't it?" Della asked Brandon right before her lips touched his.

Brandon hadn't ever laughed through a kiss, but he couldn't help it. Their lips barely brushed, and their noses bumped, then Della pulled away.

"My life is safe if that's your definition of a kiss." Justin sauntered off.

Brandon pulled Della closer and murmured, "The only reason I put up with him is because I'm nuts about you."

"Brandon?"

"Yeah?"

"What happened to your feet?"

"Have I ever remarked on how stubborn you are?"

Jordan snorted as he hung up the tuxedo he'd been wearing. "Look who's talking."

Brandon stood and pulled Della to her feet. "It's impossible to carry on a conversation around here."

Jim curled his arms around Katie. "Get used to it. Once you have a woman in your life, you'll never get a word in edgewise."

"Hey!" Katie gave him a look of mock outrage.

"You all clear out. I'll help Della load up the racks."

"Gabe, please pull the truck to the south exit." Della turned to zip a gown into a huge vinyl casing. "We won't take long."

Everyone sauntered away. Brandon held a hanger aloft as Della zipped the next gown into the protective casing. "You have this down to a fine art, and you handled that glitch like a pro."

"Thanks. I was lucky Katie's mom happened to be here and was a good sport."

"I was proud of you — you're a great emcee and came up with extemporaneous comments to make things work. You ran with it."

"Speaking of running . . ."

"Tomorrow morning. I'll pick you up at five fifteen."

"Not a chance." She looked at his feet again. "Not with those blisters. The shoes did it, didn't they?"

He'd already put her off, but the woman could teach obstinacy to a mule. At the moment, Brandon rued his promise to always be totally honest with her. "The box says size thirteen, but they're elevens."

"And you wore them? And walked around like nothing was wrong?"

"No big deal. I've had blisters that deserved birth certificates. Let's bag up that last gown."

He thought he'd distracted her until they finished packing all of the gowns and tuxedoes into the truck with Gabe's help. Della spoke to her brother, gave him a hug, and waved him off. Brandon didn't think anything of hopping into her car to go back to the shop — until she turned the wrong way.

"Don't you give me that look," she snapped.

"What are you up to?"

"I'm making sure you don't die of blood poisoning."

He decided not to argue with her . . . even

106

though the crazy woman stopped at three different places. Later, up to his ankles in a pan of Epsom salts, he ate a plate of her lasagna as she put everything back in place at the shop.

"There." She tucked away the last cummerbund and turned to him. "How are you doing?"

"Never been better. This lasagna is outrageous."

She knelt and carefully dried his feet. Brandon couldn't believe it. He didn't like anyone fussing over him; but here Della was, her classy silk dress pooling on the floor around her in wild disarray, showing him a tenderness that stole deep into his heart. He'd already mentally claimed her as his own, but the way she tended him tattled about how profoundly she cared for him, cared about him. In her own way, she was making him hers.

He wanted to grab her, hug her, and confess his love, but it was all wrong. Backward. He should be kneeling at her feet when he made that declaration. Tugging the towel from her hands, he said, "That's enough. I'm too ornery for this to bother me."

"I bought salve."

He shook his head. "Air is best. Trust me

on this."

Not even hesitating for a second, she nodded. The phone rang. "Excuse me, Brandon."

As she hurried to the phone, he bent to pick up a bag she'd set on the floor. He peered inside. Bandages, witch hazel, peroxide, Merthiolate, salve, a tube of antibiotic ointment, cotton balls — the silly woman practically bought out the drug store. But that wasn't why he smiled. She'd listened to his opinion and ignored all of her grandiose first-aid plans because she trusted him. A man couldn't ask for more — except for her heart.

"Babe," Brandon said as Della clicked her seat belt, "I've never eaten better lasagna. In fact, I've never eaten better chow, period."

She took the plate from him. "If you take me home, you can have seconds." Laughter bubbled out of her as he slammed the door and scrambled straight across the hood.

"Hey — I'm not wasting any time. I've seen how your brothers eat!" A few seconds later, Brandon shot her an exasperated look. "Stinkin' road work."

"You just complained a week ago about the potholes through here."

"That was before lasagna and your brothers were on the other end of the road!" A pained look crossed his face. "They've probably decimated the garlic bread, too."

"You already had three big slices!"

"I'd go for more, but you need a slice" — he waggled his brows — "to eat it in self-defense. Otherwise, you might not put up with me."

"I'll put up with you — anytime, anywhere."

The jeep coasted to a stop at a light. "Good thing, because you're not getting rid of me."

The certainty in his voice gave her an assurance she'd never had. Bless his heart, Brandon hadn't let her brothers or dad irritate him away. He'd accepted her as she was and taught her how to be more self-sufficient. He lived the SEAL's theme — "The only easy day was yesterday!" — and challenged her to test her own limits. Because of him, she'd discovered new strengths in herself, new abilities, new feelings.

"Truth is —" Brandon gripped the steering wheel tightly.

A loud honk made them both jump.

"Alright, alright," he groused as he stepped on the accelerator.

Della wiggled to sit sort of sideways so she could see him better. "What's the truth?"

"When I set my mind on something, I go for it."

"Yes, you're stubborn. I noticed that right away. I've never had a customer hang on to damaged merchandise and insist they still want to buy it."

"Give me a challenge, I'll rise to it."

"You'll soar past it." Della adjusted the visor to block the late afternoon sun. "You don't settle for okay — you always want stupendous."

"Like you."

"I never thought of it that way, but yes. Like me. I don't want to settle for mediocre. Funny — we're almost opposite in most ways, but in others, we're so much alike."

He shook his head. "Della, I wasn't trying to point out our similarities."

"Oh." She tugged at the shoulder belt to hide her disappointment. "Well, I sort of figured that you like me."

"I don't like you," he half-roared, "I love you!"

"He looooooooves youuuuu!" a teenaged boy in the car next to them repeated back in loud, saccharine sarcasm, then cackled and zoomed off.

"And now the whole world knows," Brandon said as he made a turn onto her street and parked in the driveway beside Justin's car. He looked her in the eyes. "I'm not sorry it does . . . but I'd planned on telling you that someplace a little more private or romantic."

Happiness flooded her. "Brandon —"

"Hey, Sis!" Gabe shouted from the porch.

She groaned.

"Later," Brandon muttered under his breath.

She nodded as Gabe continued to holler, "We're out of soda. Why don't you two go get more?"

"I have some in the trunk of my car," she called back.

A few minutes later, she and Brandon joined her dad and brothers at the table. They'd already scraped the first pan of lasagna clean. Della grabbed a spatula and rapped Justin's knuckles when he lifted his plate for more.

"Brandon?"

He grinned and slid both his plate and hers right next to the pan. "Ready when you are."

"No one's ever going to be ready for Della," Justin grumbled.

Della cut a huge chunk of lasagna and

held it over Brandon's plate. There, in front of her family, she looked at Brandon and said, "Brandon? About what you said earlier — I love you, too."

"How are the blisters?"

Brandon shoved Nathan's arm. "What's it to you?"

"Hey — I wondered if you needed a couple days' medical leave." A teasing smile lit his boss's face. "I heard they were bad."

"I wouldn't have thought Jim would blab."

"He didn't. Valene did."

"I should have guessed. Forget it. If anything, I thought maybe you'd back out on tonight." *Actually I hoped you would. I can think of a few million other places I'd rather be.*

"No way."

"Is your wife going to be okay?" Brandon took a seat in the stadium and gave Nathan a worried look. "I spotted Vanessa yesterday when I took Della to the shop. Don't take this the wrong way, but I don't like how your wife looks. I thought maybe you'd stay home with her or something."

Nathan grinned. "Nothing's wrong with Van that another eight months won't cure."

"No kidding? Congrats!"

"Thanks." Nathan beamed. "We're totally

stoked. What a blessing, you know?"

"Yeah." Brandon nodded. He couldn't help thinking of Della, picturing her all rounded with child — his child.

Things were good between them, and since they'd finally broken down and admitted their love for one another, he'd been marching around with a fool's grin plastered on his face. He'd even dared to make a few veiled references about the future. Funny, how he was usually so straightforward, but with Della, he hadn't charged ahead. Some things deserved time. The old-fashioned word *courting* came to mind.

He wanted Della to feel cherished and certain. Marriage was a forever thing. One trip down the aisle, one mate for life. As their relationship deepened, Brandon had come to the point of knowing he wanted her by his side for the rest of their lives. From their first meeting, he'd been enchanted by her, intrigued and amused . . . and each time, things got better. Never before had he used the word *love*. With Della, there was no choice — she embodied all he could ever hope for in a wife-to-be. He'd do everything possible to make her happy. And though a jog down the aisle tomorrow would suit him just fine, Brandon resolved to let this whole romance unfold in such a way that her every dream came true.

If anyone knew I was this besotted, they'd never let me live it down. He cleared his throat to cover the chuckle that bubbled up.

"So what do you think?"

Nathan's question pulled him from his musings. Brandon looked around. "Pretty hard to believe a bunch of men fill a stadium, and it's not for sports."

Nathan merely chuckled.

"This better be good," Brandon continued. He shot his boss a sideways glance. "You know I'm not into all this Holy Roller stuff."

"It's a three-night thing, and you're off the hook tomorrow and the next night if you don't want to come. No pressure."

Brandon nodded curtly. He fully expected to cash in on that provision. He'd come because Nathan wasn't just a boss — he was a friend. Since leaving the SEALs, Brandon missed the camaraderie he'd shared with his team. For six years they'd trained together, worked together, practically lived in each others' pockets. Nathan hadn't just given him work to do — he'd given him a dream job and offered his friendship. Brandon took his measure that first day and knew full well Nathan Adams was a man he could count on.

Their working relationship and friendship took on a new significance when Nathan asked him to play baseball. That little invitation gave Brandon the opportunity to bump into Della again. . . .

Yeah. One night of hellfire and brimstone. I can take it.

Brandon scanned the stadium. A platform with several microphones sat dead center of the field. A set of drums promised music of some sort. *I'd rather listen to Jesus-Loves-You music than a long-winded preacher.*

A weaselly looking guy got up and welcomed everyone. Brandon winced. There stood a man who personified his idea of a Christian man — wimpy, indecisive, needing the crutch of religion.

"I praise God for my weakness," the man said in an unsteady tone, "because in my weakness, His strength is made perfect. . . ."

Nathan murmured, "Bill was once a world-class weight lifter. He's got cancer."

Like a grenade, the words blew all of Brandon's preconceived notions to bits. The music that followed wasn't half-bad . . . until a strapping man with military bearing strode across the platform. *The guy squares his corners. Either he's still in, or he just got out.*

He got in front of the mike. Even from

the distance, Brandon could see how he grinned. "I'm sure a bunch of you men are going to pick up on this real quick. If you ever served Uncle Sam, you got a different version of the words." He paused while chuckles rumbled through the crowd. "So join in with me. . . ."

Yeah, join in. Not a chance. I haven't known a single one of these songs.

The song leader stepped back from the mike and belted out, "I don't know, but I've been told. . . ."

How many miles had Brandon marched, jogged, run with a full pack to those words? Out of sheer habit, he sang back, "I don't know, but I've been told. . . ."

"The devil's trying to keep my soul."

Well, it was a song. Brandon didn't believe the devil had much to do with his soul, but he sang along.

"Did some things, and I'm not proud. . . . Some alone, some with the crowd. . . ."

Ouch. Those words struck a cord. Brandon tried to live a good life, but he had some stuff he wished he hadn't done.

"Count 'em," the resonant cadence went on.

"One, two . . ." Brandon sang along.

"Count 'em."

"Three, four. One, two, three, four." Only

116

they weren't just words. Each number stood for something he'd done wrong. His chest went tight. A million thoughts and memories speared through his mind.

"Jesus died for all my sins. . . . I only have to ask Him in. . . . All my past is washed away. . . . All I have to do is pray. . . ."

Brandon didn't hear a word of the message. The cadence kept drumming through his mind.

ELEVEN

At the end of the evening, he walked out of the stadium and over to Nathan's truck.

Nathan slammed the door and turned to him. "What did you think?"

"Not bad. I guess I can take another night of it."

"Bet you felt right at home with Jonesy singing cadence. You belted out the words like you'd been a SEAL or something," Nathan teased.

"Yeah, or something." Brandon strove to hide behind a wry response. He had too much to think about, too much to process. They drove in silence until they passed the place he was renovating.

"Wanna show me what you've been up to here?"

Brandon grinned. "Sure."

They walked around the old building. Brandon summed up the overall accomplishments. "All the rot's gone. Had to strip

118

it down to the bones in places and completely redo it. The lines are still the same, but she's stronger, better — more functional.

Nathan nodded. "Looking great. You've proven yourself worthy of my confidence. How are we on budget?"

"It didn't come cheap. I still have work to do."

"Life's like that — the things that matter most often are the most costly."

Brandon leaned into a doorframe. "You're not talking about the project, are you?"

"If it's all you want to discuss, I am. If you feel like talking about something else, I'm available."

Brandon stayed silent. *I don't know. But I'm not a coward. I have to face this. May as well do it now as later.* "Sure your wife doesn't need you?"

"Van and Val are having a girls' night." Nathan's face scrunched into a look just short of agony. "If I go home before midnight, I'll be forced to watch old Doris Day movies."

"Fate worse than death, huh?"

"You got it. I married a great woman, but her taste in movies stinks. So believe me, you're not keeping me from anything."

Okay, Stevens. Time's up. Handle it. He

cleared his throat. "Nothing's black and white. At least, I never thought it was."

"But you're reconsidering that premise?"

Brandon nodded curtly. "Even in war, you don't just have combatants. There are neutral parties. I always figured that was me. God and the devil were welcome to duke it out, and I'd just stay clear of it all."

Nathan plopped down on a stepladder. "And now?"

"I never thought about the whole thing being polarized. A world war. You're on one side or the other. In the call-and-response, that guy singing cadence hit a nerve."

Nathan nodded.

"I've done good stuff, but I've also done things I regret. I sorta figured there's going to be a giant balance at the end of life, and as long as the good outweighs the bad, I'll get a pass into heaven. Only it's not that way, is it?"

"No, it's not. You can't be on both sides."

Brandon shook his head. "I'm not sure how to process it."

"In the end, you have to chose whom you serve."

"At what cost?" Brandon cut to the heart of the matter. "Why?"

"Because you're like this place was." Nathan swept his hand in an arc. "Parts of you are solid, but parts are rotten. If you're really going to be all you can be, you have to be willing to let God strip out the bad and rebuild you in His image. Sometimes, the process is a joy; other times, it's painful. In the end, I can promise you'll be glad of the results."

Brandon digested that analogy then said, "You didn't mention the cost."

"The cost was Christ. He paid the price. We don't have anything God wants except our hearts."

"So according to the cadence, we pray, and Jesus washes away our sins. Then what?"

"We obey." Nathan let out a long, gusty sigh. "It's not always easy. I blow it sometimes. It's not about me being perfect, though. It's about me being willing to do my best and seeking forgiveness when I blow it. I can't say what the cost is ever going to be — not for me, not for anyone else. What I do know is, God loves me and wants only what's best in the long run. Faith in His wisdom is why I obey."

Kicking the opposite side of the doorframe with the toe of his work boot, Brandon said, "Like following a superior's order, hoping he's got intel that you don't?"

"Yep." A slow smile lit Nathan's face.

"Only God is the ultimate in wisdom. You can always count on the intel when it comes down from Him."

"Slick."

"If you mean it's trite, I'm not going to try to convince you otherwise. The simplicity of salvation is undeniable."

"Black and white," Brandon said. "And I was satisfied living in the gray zone."

"Was?" Nathan studied him.

Brandon stayed quiet for a long count. When faced with truth, though, a man had to take a stand. His moment of truth had come.

"I've always viewed myself as one of the good guys. I guess it's time I joined the right side, huh? Think God would take me?"

"I know He will."

"Three nights in a row?" Della clamped the phone between her jaw and shoulder while arranging a new headpiece in the case. Tiaras and pearl-studded bands winked and glittered like promises of happily-ever-afters.

"We'll go out tomorrow night," Brandon said. "What would you like to do?"

"How about dinner and a movie?"

"Sounds great." Hammers pounded in the background. "Hang on a sec, Babe. It's too noisy in here. . . . Better now?"

"Yes. What are you doing today?"

"Jim Martinez hooked me up with a bunch of vintage molding and ceiling panels. We're installing all of it in the big rooms along the beach side of the building."

"Oh, tell me you're going to paint them all white."

"Why white?"

"Because it'll look fresh and clean and airy. . . ."

"And?" he prodded as if he knew she'd left out something. He'd gotten good at reading between the lines.

"And because I plan to book rehearsal dinners and wedding receptions there. If you chose something dreary or dark, it'll spoil everything."

He chuckled. "We couldn't have that, could we?"

"Absolutely not."

His voice went muffled for a moment, "Yeah. No. Then take it all down and redo it. It's got to be level." He cleared his throat. "Okay, Babe. Sorry. Ran into a minor disaster."

"It sounds as if you have it under control."

"Give it ten minutes. Another is bound to come up. It's been one of those days." He let out a pained chortle. "You ought to be glad we're not going out tonight. If my luck

123

held, we'd have a flat tire, and we'd contract food poisoning."

"Hold it right there! You just keep your distance then." She laughed. "Hey. Speaking of food . . . how did that pantry idea work out?"

"Great. Even got Vanessa's approval. If you have any other brainstorms, let me know."

"See? Listen to me, and even your boss's wife is happy. Would I steer you wrong?"

Brandon's deep laughter rumbled over the line, making her shiver with pleasure. "I certainly hope not."

"Consider it payback for teaching me how to bat." She sighed dramatically. "You'll probably have to teach me all over again once we start up the team after the break."

"Count on it. Those games were a great excuse to see you."

"I've missed you so much, honey." She switched the phone to her other ear and clamped it in place so she could thread a new roll of paper into the cash register.

"How much?"

Laughter bubbled out of her. "Oh, no you don't. Last time we played that game, you talked me into going on a second camping trip."

"And we had a great time. You're becoming quite the outdoorswoman."

"Well, we can't go camping this weekend anyway. My summer sale just started, and Jim and Katie are moving."

"Moving?"

"Um-hmm. He proposed at that special restaurant and everything is falling right into place for them. The apartment they wanted came vacant, so he snapped it up."

"They're going to live together?"

Della swung the little side door on the register shut, and it gave a satisfying click. She advanced the tape with several *chings* and said, "Yes. Katie's okay with it. After all, they are engaged now."

"Humpf."

"And you used to think I was so old fashioned!" Della smiled. Brandon let her know he found her more than appealing, but he never crossed the lines she set. It made her feel cherished and respected.

"You are." He paused. "And I see a lot of wisdom in those old-fashioned values."

"If nothing else, it kept us both alive. Daddy or my brothers would do something rash if we tried living together."

"Well, we have nothing to fear." The sound of his boots thumping up wooden stairs accompanied his words. "When our time comes, we're going to do everything right. Listen, Babe, I need to go. See you tomorrow."

"Okay. I love you, Brandon."

"Love you, too. Bye."

After she put down the phone, Della couldn't resist spinning in a jubilant whirl. He hadn't said *if* their time came . . . he said *when.* In the past few weeks, he'd been dropping bombs like that, and every one of them shook her world.

Brandon didn't make false promises. He didn't just blithely make comments and off-the-cuff remarks. When he said something, he meant it. He loved her. He wanted to be with her — not just for right now, but also far, far into the future. And now, he'd given her another hint that he wanted to make her his forever.

What more could a woman want?

She opened a file on the computer and looked at the newest styles. As if the computer knew all about her phone conversation with Brandon, the very first thing she saw took her breath away. There it was — the perfect wedding gown. The one she would have designed for herself. Clear down to the details on the hem, it matched everything she'd ever dreamed of. Delighted, she gazed at it and followed her impulse. She e-mailed off an order for it —

custom-made to her own measurements.

Brandon slid his arm around her shoulders and nestled Della close. "Nippy breeze tonight."

She wrapped her arm about his waist. "But you're always nice and warm."

They walked along the sidewalk, toward the park on Balboa Island. The movie they'd decided to watch was only showing at the small theater on the island, and it had been a mad dash to get there on time. He'd managed a hasty shower and changed out of his work jeans into chinos, but Della still wore one of her dress-for-feminine-success silky outfits.

Navy brass lived on and around the island. In fact, naval personnel tended to frequent the theater and restaurants here because of the quaint, intimate atmosphere. That being the case, men Brandon knew by sight, but not by name, passed by. Their gaze would go from him to Della, slow smiles would sketch across their faces, and they'd look back at him and give a nod of silent approval.

Yes, Brandon felt proud of his woman. Della was a looker — but even more, inside, she held a beauty that mattered most. Let the other guys eat their hearts out. Della belonged to him.

"Hungry now?"

She laughed. "Are you kidding?"

"I promised you supper."

"After that huge vat of popcorn?"

"That little snack?"

"If that tub were any bigger, they'd have to put it on the oceanographic charts as a newly discovered gulf of something-or-other."

"Sounds interesting. We could be the first to explore it. Have you ever gone sailing?"

"No, but I'd go anywhere with you."

His hold tightened slightly. *Thank You, God. I prayed for a chance, and this looks like a good one.* "Really? Then how about coming to church with me this Sunday?"

"You're going to church? You just went to that thing at the stadium three nights this week."

"Yeah, I did." He stopped. "I'm glad I did, too."

"Okay." She didn't bat an eye. "If it makes you happy, I'm okay with it. I can't go to church, though. I already promised Katie I'd help her unpack and hang pictures. I have to keep my word."

"Some other time. Soon." He looked at Della steadily.

"Yeah. I do go every once in a while with

Van. If I'd go with her, then you know I'd go with you."

"Thanks, Della." He kissed her softly. "That means a lot to me."

She stood on one leg and used the top of her other foot to rub the back of her calf.

"I wanted to talk with you about something important."

TWELVE

She reached up and rubbed the back of her neck. "Yes?"

Brandon brushed her hand away. "Mosquitoes eating you?"

"I don't know. I don't think so." She shuddered. "All of the sudden, I itch all over."

He tugged her under a light post. One look, and he whistled under his breath. "Babe, you've got a primo crop of hives starting. What are you allergic to?"

"Nothing."

"You'd better be, or you've got some kind of kid disease."

"I can't." She chafed her arm. "I had all my vaccinations."

He yanked out his cell phone and dialed. "Doc. Dry. My girl's got hives."

"I don't need a doctor!"

Brandon's eyes narrowed to deny her assertion as Doc started pelting him with questions. "Yeah. Breathing's fine. No, she says she's not allergic to anything. Okay. Gotcha. What kind of antihistamine?" His cell phone bugged out.

"Aargh!" Brandon dialed again, but he got no response. "Come on." He grabbed her hand and started striding toward the corner.

"Brandon!"

"Yeah?"

"You may be Daddy Longlegs, but I can't go that fast — especially in heels."

He swept her into his arms and kept walking.

"Your shoulder!"

"Is fine. Stop fussing."

She wound her arm around his neck. "What are you doing?"

"Taking you to the drug store. We're getting you an antihistamine, pronto."

"Now who's fussing?"

"I'm responding, not fussing." Traffic was light, so he didn't pause or go to the corner.

Once he stepped out into the street, Della squawked, "You're jaywalking!"

"Nope," he said as he sped up. "I'm jay-jogging."

She held on tight. "You're going to get us killed."

He stepped up on the curb and shouldered past a few pedestrians and into the drug store. "Babe, as long as you're in my arms,

131

I'll die happy."

Someone clapped him on the back. "Hey, Dry. I think that counts as PDA."

Brandon glanced over his shoulder. "I won't deny the affection, but this isn't a public display. It's an emergency."

"Man, if emergencies look like that, I'm gonna have to become a doctor like my mama wanted me to."

Della laughed self-consciously. "Hi. I'm Della."

"She has hives," Brandon tacked on as he headed down an aisle.

"Grant Luvelle." Grant followed in their wake. "Get calamine lotion. My sister always used it. She's allergic to blueberries."

Brandon stood in the middle of the aisle with Della in his arms. "Two bottles."

"You can put me down, Brandon. I can walk."

His eyes narrowed. "How are you breathing?"

"Just fine. My only problem is, I itch."

He put her on her feet, grabbed the calamine lotion, and ordered Grant, "Go get a basket and the pharmacist."

"Aye-aye!"

"Water," he muttered to himself. He raised his voice. "Lurch — toss me a bottle of water!"

Della yelped as a bottle shot through the air in a perfect spiral that would have done any quarterback proud.

"You need this to wash down the pills." He cranked off the lid in one savage wrench.

"Pills? Just how much stuff do you have in mind?"

"Whatever it takes." He scanned the shelves and started filling his arms with products that looked promising. "Hey, Lurch — what's taking so long? Where's that pharmacist?"

"*Shhh,* Brandon. I'm okay. Really." Della tried to take a box of pills from him and shove it back on the shelf.

He picked up that box again and the one next to it for good measure. "Behave yourself."

"Lurch?"

Figuring it would be a good idea to keep her distracted, Brandon nodded. "Luvelle's handle. The man can get anyone, anytime, on the radio."

Clenching her hands together to keep from itching, Della bobbed her head. "Oh, I get it — after the guy on the *Addams Family.*" She dropped her voice and intoned, "You rang?"

"Oh, man, she really must be sick if that's the best impersonation she can manage."

Lurch marched up with a white-jacketed man. "Help's arrived."

"Ahhh." The pharmacist squinted at Della and nodded. "Diphenhydramine."

"Gesundheit," Della said.

Lurch cackled. Brandon glowered at him then focused back on the pharmacist. "Do I have it?"

"No, no. It's not a disease. It's a medication."

Della got the giggles.

"I mean, do I have the dye-pen-hydrant stuff here?" He jerked his chin toward the gear he'd grabbed.

"You must. You're holding half the store," Lurch said.

Della laughed harder.

"At least you're breathing well, young lady," the pharmacist said. "That's good. Do you have any allergies?"

"Of course she does," Brandon snapped in exasperation. "Why do you think she looks like that? Let's get the show on the road here."

The pharmacist exhibited calm that would have impressed Brandon under other circumstances. Now, his demeanor only served to irritate him because the man simply wasn't sufficiently impressed with the gravity of Della's condition. "Did anything sting or bite you?" the pharmacist asked Della.

"No."

"Did you just eat anything unusual? Change to a new soap?"

Della and Brandon exchanged a look. "The —"

"— hot dog," he groaned. "Babe, I'm so sorry." Thinking the yellow stuff in the big pump-top container next to the catsup was mustard, he'd covered their hot dogs with it. Her eyes almost popped out of her head when she took her first bite. He'd teased her about having a sissy mouth, so she took a second bite before he robbed her of it, ate it, and got popcorn.

"I had some double jalapeno nacho cheese sauce," Della told the pharmacist. "Only a little."

"It doesn't take much if you're allergic." The pharmacist ignored everything Brandon gathered. He stooped, took a small box from the lowest shelf then grabbed another type of stuff from above it. "I have it in the regular and non-drowsy variety."

"We'll take both."

Della reached over and helped herself to the box that proclaimed *Non-drowsy* in screaming red letters. "I'll take one of these."

"Nope. Take the regular ones," Brandon

insisted. "You need to sleep through this ordeal. You can take the non-drowsy ones tomorrow."

"I'm not going to need them tomorrow!"

"Just in case." Brandon popped one out of the package and had her take it. He grabbed the basket from Lurch, filled it with everything he'd collected, and asked the pharmacist, "What else does she need?"

"I'm telling you, you have half the store there already," Lurch waved toward the basket. "As long as you have calamine lotion, you're set. Oh — and cotton balls. To dab it on."

"It's unnecessary." Della patted Brandon's arm. "Really, I'll be fine."

"You'll be fine," the pharmacist agreed. "But keep her hydrated."

"I have water right here." Della lifted the bottle. "He takes good care of me."

"The diphenhydramine will work shortly. Drink plenty of water and get some rest. You'll be fine, come morning."

Brandon's cell phone rang. "Yeah?" He frowned at the pharmacist. "My man said she needed to take Benadryl. Where is it?"

"She took the generic." The pharmacist scowled. "You navy guys. If you're going to call your medic, why do you bother to ask my opinion?"

"We never go in without backup," Brandon rapped out. "Thanks for the help."

"Yes, thank you," Della chimed in. "I think I feel a little better already."

Brandon snorted. "You look worse."

Lurch followed them toward the register. "Keep it up, Dry. A few more sensitive comments like that, and I'll be here to catch her when she boots you out."

"I don't wear boots," Della declared promptly. "He's stuck with me."

"You don't happen to have a sister, do you?"

"No such luck," Brandon said tersely. "Two big, ugly brothers who are almost as big a pain as you." He chucked a box of Popsicles into the basket then added Della's favorite candy bar.

Della gave up protesting. She let out a long-suffering sigh and scratched her elbow. Brandon opened the Popsicles and stuck one in her hand. "Eat that instead of itching. It's good for you."

By the time he walked her up to her door, she'd started yawning. "Is your bedroom air conditioned?"

She shook her head.

"You need a fan. Do you have a fan?"

"Ceiling fan. I'm fine, Brandon."

"You go on up and take a cool shower."

He'd already planned out the rest of the night. She'd take a shower and put on her swimsuit. He'd cover her with a whole bottle of the calamine then pour more fluids into her. After that, if her breathing was still okay, he'd let her go to sleep. On the couch. With him sitting across from her, keeping watch.

Smart. Safe.

Besides, he was scared out of his wits. Really, hives were a minor annoyance, but with Della — well, even the little things mattered a lot. *Hey, God? I'm not very good at this prayer stuff, but could You please make Della better?*

"Brandon, are you going to turn the key or not?" Della's baffled tone broke into his prayer. He nodded, and she asked, "What were you thinking?"

"I was praying."

She yawned again. "Any port in a storm."

The time wasn't right for him to tell her. He'd wanted to take time tonight to share his newfound relationship with Christ — to let her know how incredible salvation was. To invite her to discover it for herself. Then everything would be perfect.

THIRTEEN

"So Daddy threw him out at one o'clock and threatened to melt the fuse box at his place if I ever get hives on a date again." Della thrust one last book onto the shelf.

Katie laughed. "Your dad would do it, too! Here. These go on the next shelf."

"I don't know." Della accepted the next stack of books and started putting them in place. "Daddy's finally getting the idea that Brandon's going to stick around."

"I'm not looking forward to what my dad's going to say when he finds out Jim and I are living together."

Sliding a Bible onto the bookshelf, Della said nothing.

"But it's really none of his business. It's just between Jim and me," Katie said. "And we're engaged. Besides, he and Mom aren't together, so it's not like they're exactly experts on successful relationships."

Uncomfortable with the topic, Della

shrugged. "That's it for the books. I thought you wanted me to help get the kitchen set up."

"I already lined the cabinets, so we can dive right in. With all my school loans and stuff, money's tight, but I found this little dollar store that had the neatest organizers. Come on!"

Nesting . . . setting up a home of her own. Della felt a surge of excitement. Brandon mentioned Nathan's construction firm's next major project would be a housing tract. The high school retrofit and expansion had only two weeks' work to go. How long would it take to get the houses built?

"You know that plastic tub we used for a sink when we went camping? Valene got me five more from the hospital." Katie knelt by the sink. "I thought they'd be great to hold my cleaning supplies."

"Valene gets them for Vanessa to use at the pet shop, too." Della opened a small, heavy box and peered inside. "Hand me the spare ones to hold the packing peanuts around your china."

"Isn't my china beautiful? I talked Jim into buying some. We only bought four place settings because it's so expensive."

"You can list it on your wedding registry." Della carefully put the china in the cabinet

Katie indicated.

"Jim suggested we register for camping stuff. I'm not keen on the idea — I'd rather get things for our home. Who wants a tent when they don't have a bedspread? Jim surprised me. He's usually easy-going, but he dug in his heels. You know how guys are — they don't like to borrow someone else's gear."

"Brandon took me to a surplus place to get my sleeping bag. Jim can talk to him — he'd make sound recommendations on the sturdiest stuff."

Katie sat back and grinned. "You light up when you talk about him. Sounds serious to me."

"It is."

"The real thing?" Katie perked up.

"I love him with all my heart."

Brandon sat down in the gazebo in Nathan's backyard and stretched out his legs. "So when I called this morning, her dad said she was fine."

"Good." Nathan threw a battered tennis ball across the lawn for Licorice to fetch. "Jeff got hives once when we ran out of milk and I tried that powdered stuff. Didn't last long but gave me a real scare."

Licorice raced back and dropped the ball

at Nathan's feet. Nathan threw it again. "He sure misses Jeff. I do, too."

Brandon chuckled. "You just put him on the bus after church."

"But it's so quiet without him. I'm not sure he's really ready to go away to camp for a whole week."

"I'm sure you'll find stuff to fill the time. You could take Van out for a fancy supper — maybe ask Jim where he took Katie to propose. Della said it was the most romantic place around."

"Not a bad idea. As long as Vanessa's having a good day. Her morning sickness comes and goes with no rhyme or reason."

Thunk. The tennis ball landed between Brandon's feet. He leaned over, picked it up, and tossed it. "I've decided to surprise Della. I'll take her to the beach at sunrise. She'll think it's just for an early morning run. Later that evening, I'll do the candlelight dinner thing, but —"

"Wait." Nathan's smile faded. "Surprise her?"

"Yep." Brandon felt downright smug. "Ring's a beaut. Little though. Size five."

"I didn't realize you two were that serious."

"Crazy serious." Brandon chuckled. "Man, I'm not even embarrassed to admit

I'm wildly in love."

Nathan groaned as he rubbed his forehead. "Have you talked with Della about Jesus?"

"I wanted to, but the hives ruined the evening." He watched as Nathan's face went grim. "What's wrong?"

"We need to pray for Della's salvation."

"I already have."

Nathan sat in silence. Brandon could see how he struggled to frame his words. "Whatever you have to say, spit it out."

"You asked the cost of salvation."

"Yeah. And you told me Jesus paid it."

Nathan nodded. "It's only by grace that we're saved. But we also discussed obedience."

Instead of continuing to play fetch with Lick, Brandon stroked the lab. "I'm the first to admit I don't always like the rules, but I play by them. So what does this have to do with Della?"

"It means for the two of you to seek God's blessing on your marriage, you both need to be believers."

"Hold on." Brandon bolted to his feet. "My love for her isn't conditional."

"Your love isn't, but biblically, your marriage is." Nathan rose.

"You show it to me. Prove it. I don't

143

believe it."

Nathan got his Bible and leafed toward the back. He scanned a page then passed over the thick leather Bible. "Second Corinthians, chapter six."

Brandon took the Bible and started reading, *"And working together with Him, we also urge you not to receive the grace of God in vain — for He says, 'AT THE ACCEPTABLE TIME I LISTENED TO YOU, AND ON THE DAY OF SALVATION I HELPED YOU.' Behold, now is 'THE ACCEPTABLE TIME,' behold, now is 'THE DAY OF SALVATION.' "* He looked up triumphantly. "See? Now is the time. Not just for me. For Della, too."

"Man, I pray you're right — that she hears the Good News and asks Christ into her heart. But you need to read the rest of the chapter — especially the last part."

Brandon scowled. He skimmed through the next verses, then hit fourteen and fifteen. *Do not be bound together with unbelievers; for what partnership have righteousness and lawlessness, or what fellowship has light with darkness? Or what harmony has Christ with Belial, or what has a believer in common with an unbeliever?* "What's Belial?" he asked hoarsely.

"Satan."

"So if you're not with God, then you're

with the devil," Brandon said heavily. He didn't need any further explanation. There it stared back at him in black and white — it wasn't just Nathan's opinion.

"Being married means blending yourself — not just physically and emotionally, but spiritually, too. You haven't proposed yet. My advice is to pray for Della's salvation. In the meantime, asking her to marry you would be wrong."

"God wouldn't have given me Della, only to take her away."

Nathan's eyes shone with pity. "I said the same thing about Evie. She was my first wife. Died of kidney failure."

"Hey, man, I'm really sorry. But if your point is that God gave you Vanessa and you're happy, that's fine — it's your story." Brandon's throat ached with the strain of trying not to shout. "I'm not going to be happy with anyone else. I don't want anyone else. I love *her*."

"I've missed you so much!" Della dove off the porch and into Brandon's arms. His arms closed tightly around her, and his head dipped, but he didn't kiss her. Della understood. Affection belonged between them, not as a show for others.

"Get her out of here, will you?" Daddy

145

groused. "She's been moping ever since her hives spoiled that date."

Brandon set her down.

"I'm sorry. Did I hurt your shoulder?" She reached up to rub the place where a wicked scar sliced from beneath the edge of his tank top.

Brandon grabbed her hand and twined their fingers. "I'm fine."

Della didn't say anything more about it. He refused to admit it ever bothered him and hated to be reminded of his injury. "So where are we going?"

"To The Spindles."

She did a hop-skip beside him. "Is it official? Nathan approved?"

"Yes. Vanessa says it's a perfect name, too. I'm even having a sign painted."

Della beamed. "When you started putting all of that fancy gingerbread trim back on, the name just came to me. It sounds elegant. Old fashioned."

"It's been a challenge to match some of that woodwork." Brandon talked about the renovation and a few little things he planned to do in order to complete the project. "Just the finishing touches," he said. "Then we're going to have an open house. We're already getting calls about booking meetings and conferences."

"You need to have a 'No Red Punch' policy. Red punch stains carpeting and floors."

"Good idea." He flashed a smile at her. "Anything else?"

"Not that I can think of offhand." They rounded a corner, and she caught her breath. "Oh, Brandon! The landscaping is done!"

"Like it?"

"I love it! That little arbor off to the side looks inviting, and the fountain! Oh, look at it!"

He chortled. "If I never see another fountain again, it'll be too soon. I must have looked at five hundred of them to find the one that looked okay."

"Well, you found just the right one." She hopped out of the jeep and stuck her hand into the cool water. "Take a picture of this view and have postcards made."

"I already took a picture for the website. Come look inside." He chafed her wet hand to dry it off. "I wanted to put in cobblestones, but they're too dangerous. Someone would twist an ankle and sue."

He opened the door.

"*Oooh,* Brandon!" Della crossed the threshold and stepped into the center of the entryway. Slowly turning to take in the

147

whole view, she didn't even want to blink. "It's incredible!"

"Vanessa and her mom met with an interior decorator. I gave them a basic list of essentials. What do you think of the furniture?"

"Ellen always has impeccable taste. It's elegant, but inviting. Some of the styles from that period were stuffy, but this — it just oozes 'Welcome!' "

They went from room to room and finally ended up back at the entry. Brandon led her over to a window seat. During the tour, Della kept sensing something was up. She didn't want to rush him. By the time she sat down, she could hardly stay put. Suddenly, his behavior made sense. She couldn't have asked for a more romantic place to receive a proposal.

Smiling up at him, she patted the cushion beside herself.

Brandon sat then stood back up again. Della didn't want to spoil the moment by laughing at him. It had to be nerve-racking for a man to summon the courage to ask a woman to marry him.

Not that he had any reason to worry that she'd refuse.

"Babe, I brought you here because I came to the most important decision of my life in this room. I hope you will, too."

His eyes went the color of buffed pewter, and he gently cupped her hand in his.

Her heart filled to overflowing.

FOURTEEN

"Give my heart to Jesus?" she echoed his words in disbelief.

Brandon nodded. "Yes. I used to think being good was enough. It's not. I can't do it on my own merits. Christ died for me. Accepting that fact is the only way I'll ever make it to heaven."

Della snatched her hand from his.

Brandon's heart twisted. He could see the confusion in her eyes. "Let me explain." He crouched on the floor in front of her. "God loves you."

"Well, since He does, then He won't damn me to hell."

"No, Babe. It doesn't work that way."

She drew back from him. "Brandon, if you're happy with doing the whole church-and-Jesus thing, that's fine by me. You've never asked me to compromise on things that matter most to me. I won't ask that of you, either."

Lord, this isn't going how I wanted it to.

"I'll even go to church with you some-times. You already know that."

"It's not just a behavior. It's a change inside," he tried to explain.

"I'll love you, no matter how you change." Hurt shone in her eyes. "Why do I have to change just to suit you?"

"It's not just to suit me. I love you, no matter what."

Her chin lifted. "Then I don't see what the fuss is about."

"I love you with my heart. I love God with my soul."

Her brows puckered. "It's not some kind of competition."

He shook his head sadly. "No, it's not. Listen, I'm not trying to be pushy. I wanted to share something precious with you be-cause I love you."

"Well, you shared it. I'm happy for you." Her smile looked forced. "So what else did you want to do today?"

He'd hoped she'd see the truth and re-spond, but how many times had he heard the salvation message and not taken action? Being forceful would only push her away. She'd closed the subject, and he'd play along for now. There would be plenty of chances for him to witness to her. Brandon twirled a lock of her hair around his finger. "What would you like to do?"

She thought for a moment. "Why don't we go to Balboa Park and wander around the museums?"

"Only if you promise we won't get lost in the Aerospace Museum." He tugged on that tress. "Last time, I never got to the Timken."

Della laughed. "How was I to know you liked fine art more than a bunch of military artifacts? I was trying to make sure you enjoyed yourself."

"Babe, I could lead you through that place blindfolded. I spent almost every weekend of my early teens there. The day we went there, I was far more interested in the woman by my side than anything on display."

"And when we get into the Timken, will you still feel that way?" She batted her lashes.

"Hmmm," Brandon teased. "I don't know. That place is small, but the pieces they have on display are incredible. You, on the other hand . . ."

"Brandon!"

He grinned. "Gotcha!" He winked. "In my eyes, you are God's greatest work of art."

Signing her name with a flourish, Della accepted the shipment. From the label, she knew exactly what it contained: her dress! Of all times for it to arrive, why now? She had a nitpicky mother of the flower girl who didn't like the dress the bride had chosen for the little girl to wear. It took every shred of Della's diplomacy to deal with the woman and her whiny daughter even before the interruption of the shipment's delivery. Now, all she really wanted to do was shoo them out, flip over the OUT FOR LUNCH sign, and relish the sight of her very own wedding gown.

But that wasn't professional. She tamped down her wishes, bumped the box toward the back of the shop, and returned to her customers.

"Let's have Audrey try on the dress," she said brightly. "It's one of those styles that always looks so much cuter on."

"But it's pink," her mother repeated for the third time as she smoothed her hand down her daughter's copper-red hair.

"Yes, and it's very feminine." Della tried to turn what had been intended as a flaw into a selling point.

"I want my daughter to wear white."

"You mentioned that on the phone," Della said in her most diplomatic tone. "But the bride insists on all of the party wearing pink."

"I like pink, Mommy," Audrey whined.

"Well, then, this is just right!" Snagging the dress from the hook, Della slipped between mother and child and nudged her into a dressing room. "You're a big girl, Audrey. Why don't you put this on, and we'll have Mommy keep her eyes closed when you come out. I'll zip you up and stand you on that platform over by the big mirror, just like the brides do when they model their gowns."

"Yeah!" Audrey couldn't shut the door fast enough.

Looking thoroughly disgruntled, her mother muttered, "Pink," and headed for the rack of children's-sized formalwear.

Usually, brides came in and were part of this event. In this case, the bride intentionally skipped being present for the fitting. She'd confessed to Della that the little girl was sweet as could be, but nothing ever pleased the mother.

No novice to such circumstance, Della knew how best to handle things. She had suggested the bride give the mother some nominal choices regarding the accessories. "Anything," the bride had begged, "just get Audrey in the dress!"

Della approached the mother. "It'll take Audrey a little time."

"She's only seven. I don't know why you think she can get into that dress by herself."

"I'm sure it'll be difficult." Della nodded agreement and cast a glance over her shoulder then lowered her voice conspiratorially. "That's why I have her try here. It'll make her glad to have your help on the Big Day."

"Oh. Yes. Good."

A little soprano called out, "I can't do up the zipper thing. Mommy, don't look!"

Della winked at the mother, who suddenly became an ally.

"I'll wait over here, honey."

"Actually," Della paused then pointed toward a display case — the one she and Brandon met at. "The bride left it to your discretion whether Audrey wears gloves. I have both lace and cotton ones, if you think she should wear them. Why don't you take a quick peek?"

Della zipped up Audrey's dress, led her to the platform, and smiled as the little girl squealed in delight at her reflection. "Let's make sure everything is just right before —"

"Oh, Audrey!"

"Aren't I pretty, Mommy?"

Della held her breath.

"Honey, you are beautiful. Just look at

you!" Her mother drew closer.

By the time they left, Audrey's mother couldn't stop gushing. "I love pink. People always told me redheads couldn't wear it, so I didn't buy any for Audrey. I can't believe how silly I was. The truth was right in front of me, and I never saw it!"

As soon as she shut and locked the door, Della flipped over the sign and dashed toward the box. She'd no more than picked it up when someone started banging on the door. Letting out a resigned sigh, she set down the box and turned around.

"Della!" Vanessa stood there, rapping on the glass like a demented woodpecker.

"I'm coming."

"No!" Vanessa shouted through the glass. "Hurry! Go shut off the electrical main!"

Since their shops adjoined, they shared the same box. It took a lot to rattle Vanessa, so Della reacted at once. She ran through the shop, out the back, and over to the fuse box. Once she shut down the power, she dashed back to Vanessa.

"What —"

"Oh, you'll never believe it," Vanessa used her fingers to squeegee water out of her hair.

"It's you. Of course I'd believe it."

"I'd just finished grooming Mrs. Rosetti's terrier. She's such a dear. So is her dog.

Anyway, I went into the back to rinse out the tub, and the faucet broke."

"So . . ." Della ventured slowly, "you want me to call a plumber?"

"No, I'll have Nathan come fix it. I need you to call your dad. When the faucet broke, I had it on full blast. The shower massage thing turned into a bullwhip. It jerked out of my hands."

"You're okay? You didn't slip?"

"I'm fine."

Envisioning the five-foot-long fiberglass hose still wreaking havoc, Della headed back through the shop. "I'll turn off the water main, too. What about Mrs. Rosetti's dog?"

"She took him home before it happened," Vanessa called. "Hey, you don't have any towels in your back room, do you?"

All the years of listening to her brothers and father didn't help. They'd never let her come close when they were working. Brandon, on the other hand, had commented on the shared utilities one night when they'd left the shop. Because of him, Della knew where the shut offs were.

She snagged a cordless phone and a linen tablecloth as she headed back to Vanessa. Once she'd wrapped Van in the tablecloth, Della froze. "I didn't think — are you sure you're okay? Van, with all of the wiring you

157

have for the radiant heaters, you could have electrocuted yourself!"

"I'm fine. Really. Your dad insisted on the rubber floor mats. They probably saved my life. I jumped out of there and came running for help." She let out a weak laugh. "I don't think I've ever prayed so hard, so fast!"

Della knew Nathan and her dad were both supposed to be at The Spindles today. She called Brandon. She'd no more than started to explain what had happened when he boomed, "Are you okay?"

"Yes. It was at Van's —"

"Is Van all right?"

"Yes —"

A tussle sounded, and Nathan's voice came over the phone. "Van — is —"

"She's right here." Della handed her the phone. Three minutes later, while Vanessa was still talking to her husband, Brandon's jeep screeched to the curb. He and Nathan bolted from it as Daddy's truck rounded the corner and skidded to a halt. The fact that two police cars pulled up behind with lights and sirens only added to the effect.

Brandon grabbed Della and held her tight. Her dad stood behind her, yanking her back toward him. In the midst of their tug o' war, Della watched as Nathan scooped up Van-

158

essa — tablecloth, phone, and all, and plowed toward a cruiser.

"Sir —"

"My wife just about got electrocuted. Get us to the hospital." The one squad car left.

Della remained sandwiched between Brandon and her father as the other officer approached. "You men were speeding."

Brandon yanked Della closer still. "I was going faster."

"I don't understand how anything so right can be wrong." Brandon could barely get the words past the tightness in his throat.

Nathan squeezed his shoulder — the bad one. The pain didn't even begin to compare with the anguish Brandon felt.

They stood at the head of the stairs, looking down as the caterer carried the last bag of trash away.

Della, radiant in a russet-colored dress, thanked the worker as Vanessa closed the door. The women shared an exuberant hug. "Oh, it's been a splendid affair!"

"Everyone loves it," Vanessa agreed. "I'll bet Nathan has this place booked solid for the next six months!"

The two women chattered and headed for the kitchen.

Brandon gripped the banister until his

nails dug grooves in the highly polished oak. "I love her."

"I know you do," Nathan said in an equally muted tone.

"We're opposites on just about any level. She's a princess; I'm a jock. She's — well." He groaned. "It works for us. We're a perfect fit. Why can't we be different about God?"

Nathan jerked his head toward one of the upstairs business suites. They went in, shut the door, and sat across from one another in the made-for-big-men upholstered chairs. The silence between them ached.

Finally, Nathan asked, "Have you prayed about it?"

"I have. I can't. I do." Brandon banged his fist on the arm of his chair. "God must be sick of hearing me. I've been begging Him for three weeks solid."

"God isn't sick of hearing you. He'd love to have Della as His daughter. Ultimately, she has to make the decision, though."

"What's so wrong about me marrying her? I'd get her to come to church. She'd hear the gospel. I can't see anything wrong with that."

"It's tough." Nathan winced. "But you're assuming a lot — that she'll eventually make a decision to follow Christ."

"She has to."

"There aren't any guarantees. We live by what we value. Since you've been saved, you're using your time differently. Can you honestly say that Della wouldn't be jealous of the time you spend alone in the Word and in prayer? You said she's uncomfortable when you pray at meals now."

"She could get used to it." Brandon resented the question. He resented the need for the question. Why couldn't Della just see the light?

"You don't marry with the expectation of changing your mate. You have to say your vows with the understanding that you fully accept Della as she is. It'll make for an unhappy marriage if she feels like she doesn't measure up to your expectations or hopes."

Nathan's words held a lot of wisdom.

Brandon didn't want to think about it though. Given enough time, surely, Della would have to . . . but his thoughts came to a grinding halt. Wishing for something didn't make it happen.

"And what about your children? You'll want to dedicate them to the Lord and train them up to know Him." Nathan's words hit hard. "A mother's example is vital."

Brandon raked his fingers through his hair. "I can't make this decision. Not yet."

"Hey, you guys!" Vanessa's voice cut into the conversation. "Stop hiding away and gloating alone. You promised to take us out for a celebration dinner!"

Nathan popped to his feet and headed toward the door. He cast a quick glance back at Brandon. "Take a minute." He left and shut the door.

Brandon could hear Della's heels clicking up the wooden stairs. Every beat sounded just like a nail being driven into a coffin.

"Guess which fork," Della teased as dessert arrived. They'd gone out to supper with Vanessa and Nathan — an elegant dinner at a fabulous restaurant. Nathan and Brandon both complained about the "arsenal" of silverware on the table, but neither had a bad thing to say about the wonderful food and service.

Brandon didn't pause for a moment. He reached over and swiped hers. "This one."

Laughter bubbled out of her. Brandon's playfulness cropped up at the most unexpected times, but whenever it did, it never ceased to delight her. She held out her hand.

His brow hiked in unspoken challenge.

"That's cheating." She wiggled her fingers in a beckoning motion. "I know you always play by the rules."

"You can share," Vanessa suggested.

"Are you kidding?" Nathan gave his wife a disbelieving look. "Della ordered chocolate cream pie. No man in his right mind deprives a woman of chocolate."

Brandon laid the fork back in Della's hand. The silver felt warm from his touch. "Truer words were never spoken. Get this: Della keeps a stash of chocolate behind the cash register."

"With all of those expensive gowns?" Nathan gave Van an astonished look. "Did you know that?"

"Of course she did." Della gave the men a you-have-to-be-kidding-me look. "Girlfriends don't hold out on one another."

"In fact, Della invited me over to taste test the chocolates." Vanessa grinned. "We decided on the best ones."

Brandon gave Nathan an I-told-you-so look. "Women and their chocolate."

"Since when did you care about chocolate?" Della tapped the back of his hand with her fork. "When we went hiking, you took away my chocolate and made me carry beef jerky!"

"Chocolate melts. The sugar attracts insects. It's a refined carbohydrate, so you don't get long-term energy from it."

"See?" Della cast a knowing look at Vanessa. "He not only plays by the rules, he can quote them." The waiter served the desserts. Della cut a bite of her chocolate cream pie and held it up to Brandon's mouth. "I'm going to tempt you. Forget the rules and live a little."

His eyes darkened, and for a moment, Della had the strange feeling she's said something wrong. Embarrassment swept over her. Had they mistaken her words to mean something racy?

"Oh, eat that." Vanessa picked up her own fork and dug into her mud pie. "Della, just don't blink, or Brandon will inhale his pie and yours."

Everyone chuckled, but the tension didn't dissipate. Della couldn't shake the odd sensation that she was missing something important, but she didn't want to ruin the supper by asking. This was Brandon's big day. He'd proven his skills by completing a detailed, difficult renovation. Nothing was going to dampen the joy.

"Something's wrong," Della said as they sat in the cool sand the next morning. Tendrils of early morning fog swirled around them, but they'd finished their run and were warm.

Only Brandon's blood ran cold. "What do

you mean?"

She shrugged. "I don't know. I can't figure it out. Everything used to be so easy between us. Suddenly, it's strained. I don't get it."

The time's come. Brandon whispered a prayer for a miracle . . . and if that miracle didn't happen, for the strength to do what he had to. He reached over and folded her hand in his.

FIFTEEN

"I've changed, Della. I'm a new man." The confused look in her eyes had him continue, "When you accept Christ, you're a new person."

"Don't be ridiculous. You're the same man."

"No, Babe, I'm not. I've come to know the Lord, and that makes me different — different from who I used to be, and" — he paused and added quietly — "different from you."

A wariness crossed her features. "I told you that doesn't matter to me. I'll do the church thing with you sometimes."

"That's a good start, and I appreciate that you're willing to meet me halfway."

"But?" Her voice nearly broke on that one syllable.

"But it's not enough. Some things in life can't be halfway."

"What are you saying, Brandon? That if I

don't get religious, I'm not good enough for you?"

"I'm not religious, Babe. What I am is forgiven."

"You're a good person. So am I. We had this talk and agreed that was enough. Suddenly, you're changing the rules, and I have to change or I don't measure up? Give me a break, Brandon. Those rules don't matter. Christians don't even keep their own rules. Look at Katie and Jim — they're Christians, and they're living together."

"We both know they shouldn't." He didn't know how to respond to her comment. For people to call themselves Christians and live against God's precepts didn't just affect their own lives. It also ruined their witness. The pastor had a term for that — being a stumbling block. How could non-Christians understand what it meant to be different — to be set apart, when Christians acted just like non-Christians?

He let out a big sigh. "The wrong things others who call themselves Christians do make me sad, and I can't condone their actions."

"So if they do something wrong and God still loves them, then He can still love us. We're not even doing anything."

"There are going to be times when I blow

it. I'm not saying I'm perfect. But when I do mess up, I'll go to the Lord and ask forgiveness and try to follow Him more closely. I'm responsible for my own behavior."

"But you're not responsible for my decisions. Just because I don't wear a cross and sing hymns, it's not your fault."

"Being a Christian isn't just something you do; it's what you are on the inside."

"Well Katie and Jim say they're Christians. I don't see any difference. Why are they any better than I am? I'm not sleeping with you. I haven't done anything wrong." Tears filled her big brown eyes. "You want me to buy into this whole God-and-religion thing, and I don't. All of a sudden, who I am isn't good enough for you. I can't lie, Brandon. So we have this — this" — she slashed her hand up and down — "this *wall* between us. I didn't put it there. You did. Isn't my love for you enough?"

Pain washed over him, lapped and pulled at him like the outgoing tide. He cupped her cheek. "Babe, you're the only woman I've ever loved. You're the only woman I'll ever love — but I can't lead you on."

"You're not leading me on. I know what the score is. We're different in lots of ways, but we get along just fine."

"This is the one thing that's not negotiable. I'll wait for you. I'll pray for you. But I can't keep dating you or ask you to marry me until you've given your heart to Jesus."

She sat there in stunned silence. Slowly, her eyes filled and huge tears began to roll down her cheeks. "You don't mean that."

God, help me. He rasped, "I do."

She fell apart on him. Brandon held her as she soaked his T-shirt with her tears. Some of his joined hers. He'd made the decision because it was the only honorable and righteous thing to do — but the anguish was unbearable. The depth of Della's emotions only plunged the dagger more deeply into him. He'd done this — and he couldn't do a thing to change it.

"I can't believe it," Della told Katie two days later. "Van and Val were my best friends in high school. We were all still so tight — and then poof! They just side with Brandon."

"That's rough," Katie sympathized.

"I still can't believe it. We were so right together. Everything went like a fairy tale; then he just dumped me."

The ice clinked in their glasses as Della wiped away her tears. "Van spouted off something about him being a Christian so

169

we'd be 'unequally yoked,' as if we're stupid oxen."

"Oh, yeah." Katie nodded. "Now I get it." She hastily held up her hands. "Don't get me wrong. I think it stinks. You and Brandon make a great pair."

"So then what's the problem? He can go to church. I already promised him that. What more does he want?"

Trailing the tip of her fingernail in a water drop on the tabletop, Katie sighed. "From what Jim's said, Brandon's a play-things-by-the-book sort of guy. Christians make rules. They think there's only right and wrong — nothing in between. That leaves you here." She made a wet dot on one side of the water streak on the table, "and him here." She made another dot on the opposite side then looked up.

"You and Jim aren't like that. You accept me just the way I am. Why can't God? Why can't Brandon?"

"God will accept you — but there's a hook. You have to accept Him as your personal Lord and follow Him. That's what Brandon wants out of you, too."

"Why can't you Christians get your story straight? You're a Christian. You aren't forcing me to agree with you or be damned to hell."

Katie shrugged. "I'm not hard-core Christian. I was once — back in high school. But life happens, you know? My parents split up, and God didn't make it better. I still believe in Jesus, but I don't feel like I have to walk around quoting the Bible and show up in church every time they open the doors."

"Then I don't see the difference." Della couldn't hold back the tears. "I figure God is there somewhere, too. Why should I have to conform to their rules just so I'm good enough to love?"

Squirming in her seat, Katie shrugged. "I don't know."

"Stevens."

Brandon glanced up from the blueprints and knew he was in for a rough time. Della's dad and brothers looked ready to electrocute him. "Yeah."

"I told you back at the start, if you made my baby girl cry, I'd —"

Brandon nodded once, curtly. He didn't need to hear the threat. If having the Valentine men beat him to oblivion would solve the problem, take away Della's pain, or mute his own, Brandon would willingly stand still and let them take him down.

"You hurt her." Gabe's accusation hung

in the air.

"I know." He didn't bother to hide the ache in his voice.

"You love her," Justin ground out. "We all know you do."

Brandon looked him in the eye. "I can't deny that. But it's not enough."

"Not enough?" Della's father bellowed in outrage.

"Sir, I respect your daughter. I can't ask her to change."

"My daughter is perfect. She doesn't need to change."

"I've accepted Christ as my personal Savior. Because of that, I'm not the same man I used to be."

"You're no man at all to hurt my sister," Justin sneered.

"I'd hurt her every day by wishing she were something she isn't. I can't do that to her." Brandon rested his palms on the table. "I told her I'd pray for her. That I'll wait. I'll have faith that someday —"

"Forget it." Gabe slashed the air. "Just forget it. Della doesn't need you and your religion. It's you who's not good enough for her."

Nathan sauntered up. "Gentlemen?"

Della father shook his finger at Brandon. "As long as he works for you, I don't. Power

Electric is canceling our contract bid on the housing development."

"I'm sorry you feel that way. I value Brandon."

"You made your choice." Della's family stalked off.

Brandon stared down at the blueprint. It was the one he'd chosen as the home he'd buy for his future with Della. No matter where he turned, reminders of his loss swamped him. He rasped, "I thought God was supposed to give me peace about this."

"This is a different kind of war. Peace doesn't mean an absence of struggle. It means you're certain that no matter what happens, God wins in the end."

"Ultimately, God wins the war, but I never wanted to put Della in the line of fire. What kind of man am I to let the woman I love become a battle casualty?"

"You're a man of faith," Nathan stated firmly. "God can bind every wound and heal the brokenhearted. Put your trust in Him."

Brandon thumped a weight down on a fluttering end of the blueprint. "I used to think only weak men turned to God. I'm coming to discover it takes more strength to believe than to deny Him."

"I'm sure he's a nice guy, but —"

"Oh, come on." Katie yanked on the cord to close the blinds in her apartment then nudged one of Jim's shoes toward the corner, next to the backpack overflowing with her new textbooks. "You have to quit moping, Della. I already told Harvey all about you. We'll double-date. You can chose where you want to go. Saturday night —"

"I'm already busy Saturday night." Della jumped on the opportunity to avoid another of Katie's matchmaking attempts. "I know you're trying to help me, but I need some time."

"I can't help it if I know dozens of guys. I'm surrounded by them in school. Brainy, hunky engineering and architectural majors. You could do a lot worse."

Della didn't respond. Katie had a habit of asserting herself, and most of the time it was okay, but this wasn't one of those times. After Manny just "happened" to run into them at a movie, Della didn't say anything. It felt like a set-up, but she didn't want to make unfounded accusations. Lunch with Ashley seemed like a nice break — until Ashley turned out to be "a true Southern gentleman" with an obsessive need to cut his sandwich into precise, one-inch squares.

"It'll be fuuuuu-unnnn," Katie sing-songed.

"I told you, I already have plans."

"You're serious!" Landing on the sofa with a pounce, Katie squealed. "Tell me all about it."

"I'm going on a weekend hike."

"You? Hike?" Hysterical laughter poured out of her. "I've been camping with you. You could barely make it with" — she caught herself — "all of our help."

"I'm an independent woman. Whatever I don't have in ability, I make up for in effort."

Looking thoroughly unconvinced, Katie squirmed for a minute then brightened. "Oh, I get it. You know with skiing how they have the little bunny hills and the advanced runs? You're just going to do one of the little ones, right?"

"No. It's a real hike. Five days."

"Five days!" Katie gawked at her as if she'd lost her mind.

Della nodded with far more confidence than she felt. "It's real camping. Pup tents. Boots and backpacks and marshmallows." Memories of toasting marshmallows and snuggling by Brandon at the campfire threatened to swamp Della. She straightened her shoulders and suppressed the memories. "My boots are broken in, and I'm great at toasting marshmallows. I'll do just fine."

"You're going to break your neck." Katie shook her head. "I've never heard a more ridiculous idea in my life."

"Hey — where's the support? Friends are supposed to cheer you on, not knock you down."

"Friends," Katie said in a doomsday voice, "are supposed to stop you when you're doing something dumb." She pulled a throw pillow onto her lap and hugged it. After a pause, she asked quietly, "Does anyone else know you're doing this?"

Della knew she meant Brandon, but she purposefully ignored the thinly veiled question. Pasting on a cheerful smile, she proclaimed, "Ellen Zobel is watching the shop for me. She always does such a great job. I don't know if she's told Van or Val. That whole clan sits together in church, so they'll find out soon enough."

"I don't think this is such a bright idea."

"I'll be fine. I'm going with a group — Rugged Adventure."

"Never heard of them. Did you check them out?"

Della leaned back into the sofa. Finally, a question that didn't feel like the Spanish Inquisition! "I looked all over. You know me and the Internet. I narrowed it down to three different companies, and this one is close-by and had an opening for dates that Ellen could cover the shop for me. It worked out perfectly. You should see their brochure on the Internet."

Katie waggled her brows. "Are the guides hunks?"

"You're impossible." Della swallowed one last sip of coffee then stood. "I need to get going. I have a lot to do." After giving Katie a hug, she ran a few errands before heading home.

Sitting at the curb was Brandon's jeep.

Sixteen

Brandon knew the minute she drove up. Her brothers and dad had been in the garage when he arrived. They came out to "greet" him. Their idea of hospitality left a lot to be desired. He put up with it though. Della was more important than their anger.

Brandon ignored Gabe's latest snarl and looked right over the fuming man's shoulder to see Della slide from her car. Dainty heels. Swirly lavender dress. Big, hurt eyes.

His heart wrenched.

She turned to go into the house.

Brandon took a step forward.

The Valentine men formed a wall.

Brandon didn't want to fight them. It would be ugly. All three would be in a bloody heap in a few seconds.

"Della, I need a minute with you."

"Nobody here cares what you want," Mr. Valentine roared. "Della needs you to get out of here."

Slowly, Della turned. She refused to look Brandon in the eyes. "Say what you came to say."

It didn't escape his notice that she hadn't come within several feet. Her vulnerability tore at him. Brandon wanted nothing more than to shove her family apart and gather her into his arms, but he didn't have the right. He cleared his throat.

"The hike you're going on — it's not safe." In revealing that, he knew she'd realize someone had talked with him about her. She didn't need to know who. Fact was, Ellen told Van and Val, who both told their husbands. Jordan and Nathan discussed it, and Nathan came to him. He hadn't known the details, though, until Katie called him. Della didn't have a clue that so many people truly cared about her.

Since they'd broken up, she'd withdrawn from almost everyone. Van and Val both said once Della knew they supported his decision on a biblical basis, she'd avoided them.

She held her purse like a shield. "I'm going."

"It's not safe, Della." He strove to reason with her, but from the way she hung back and stared off at nothing warned him she wasn't receptive to what he came to say. Still, he had to try. "I checked into it. Rug-

ged Adventure is a two-bit, seat-of-the-pants
—"

"Rugged Adventure is a business. They
know what they're doing."

He changed tactics. "Then I'll go along.
Just as a friend. Just to be sure —"

"No." She finally looked him in the eyes.
"You're not my friend. I could never be just
friends with you. Leave me alone, Brandon."
She pivoted and headed toward the porch.

Brandon watched as her shoulders began
to shake. She'd started weeping, and he was
powerless.

Thump.

Air whooshed out of him from being
sucker punched. Brandon didn't defend
himself.

Justin glowered and kept his fists raised.
"You made her cry."

"I'm more sorry than you'll ever know."
Brandon got into the jeep and left. He went
to the beach and ran several miles. The
steady beat of feet pounding the sand didn't
bring oblivion. All it did was punctuate the
unending waves of grief at having hurt the
only woman he'd ever love.

Finally, he walked to cool down and sat in
the icy solitude of the star-blanketed beach.
*God, don't let her hurt like this. Do whatever it
takes. If she's never going to come to You,*

then let her fall in love with someone who will make her happy. I'll take the pain. I'll handle the loneliness. Just please, God — don't make Della pay for my decision to follow You.

"We'll make camp here tonight."

Della watched in disbelief as Chet unbuckled his backpack and let it drop to the ground. The guide chose a lousy location. They were close to water — too close, because the water wasn't moving much at all. It smelled brackish. The clearing was large enough to handle their group, but the ground sloped. The wind cut through at a nasty angle, too.

Ten other hikers struggled out of their gear. Della decided not to give her opinion. Resigned to slapping on extra bug repellant, she decided to position herself between other tents so they'd serve as nominal windbreaks.

Chet sauntered up. "Della, you'll be with Misty and Madeline."

"I thought you said they're two-man tents," she said.

He studied her from head to foot and shrugged. "Man. You're all woman, and —"

"Hold it right there." She glowered at him.

"Hey, I'm not trying to come onto you or anything." He waved his hand as if to erase the words. "I meant to say, you're all women. The other two are small. Three of you'll fit fine."

She didn't say another word. He'd gotten the message that she wasn't about to put up with any flirting. Still, just about the last thing she wanted was to share a tent with the two bickering teens. The sisters didn't want to be here, and they'd made no secret of that fact. If tonight went badly, Della decided she'd have cause to ask for a reassignment. For now, she wanted to put up the tent and eat.

Rugged Adventure outfitted its hikers — but for a small fortune. Della had borrowed Gabe's backpack and brought her own sleeping bag and hip mat. A trip to the surplus place filled in the rest of the essential gear. Seeing the poor quality of the others' sleeping bags made her glad she'd seen to her own equipment.

"Tents!" the other worker shouted as he dropped bundles every few feet. The fact that one of the employees carried the tents had seemed like a great idea. Della didn't feel capable of toting the additional weight. Now that she saw the flimsy nylon structures, she consoled herself with the fact that California Septembers weren't especially cold. They'd brought five, two-man tents.

With ten campers, two workers . . . The math simply didn't add up.

"I guess we'd better pitch this thing," Della said to Misty.

"The only thing Misty is pitching is a fit," Madeline said as she kicked the small bundle.

"All I care about is having a warm, dry place to sleep." Della methodically opened the bundle and started fitting together the fiberglass framing poles. The girls disappeared, so she ended up doing the work by herself. Once she had the tent up, Della started driving in stakes.

Chet came over. "Here. I'll do the rest." He took a stake, shoved it straight down into the ground, and banged on it with a hammer.

It's wrong. It should go in at an angle, just like Brandon showed me. Especially with the wind, we'll need it secured. "I can do this. Really. Why don't you help someone else?"

"Not a problem. It'll only take a minute." He flashed her a smile. "Besides, it gives me an excuse not to cook."

"What's for supper?"

"Shish kabobs. Packed 'em frozen, and they'll be thawed and ready to stick on the fire."

"Sounds good. I'm hungry." She smiled,

even though he pounded in another stake the wrong way.

Supper tasted great. The day's activity and cool air sharpened her appetite. Della decided the trip was working out well enough. There were bound to be a few glitches here and there, but for the most part, the group seemed happy. A few songs at the campfire, rich hot chocolate, and they turned in for the night. Misty and Maddy both argued about the limited space. They complained about the hard ground.

Della wished she'd brought earplugs. She burrowed into her sleeping bag and tried to ignore them. Then she decided she'd wished they hadn't fallen asleep. At least their arguing served as a diversion. Now she couldn't stop the flood of memories from the times Brandon took her camping.

The wind howled. Someone snored. The corner of the tent lifted and started flapping. Della fought the crazy urge to laugh because she couldn't decide whether it was the wind or the snore that blew it loose. In her heart, though, she knew if Brandon had tacked down that stake, it wouldn't have given way.

They hiked farther into the San Bernardino Mountains the next day and made good time. At one point, they passed through a vacant campground. Della drank at a fountain then refilled her canteen. She wondered why they didn't set up for the night here, but Chet clapped his hands. "Gather up. We still have plenty of light. No sissy camping. We're stouthearted adventurers. Open trail for another hour or so before we stop."

"Well, there's truth in advertising," someone said in a wry tone. "This is definitely a 'rugged adventure.' "

Folks laughed and fell into step. They chattered along the path, but Della couldn't help remembering how Brandon was as he hiked — he'd point out types of trees, plants, rocks. Interesting little facts. According to what Brandon taught her, Chet led them out of the chaparral, past the yellow pine forest, and crossed through montane meadows. From what she could judge, they'd come to the lodgepole forest. But Chet didn't talk about the different geological regions or point out the tracks in the earth from deer or raccoons. He just plowed on ahead. Compared to her hikes with Brandon, this so-called adventure was nothing more than a harsh march.

Chet consulted the GPS then adjusted their course when a rockslide obliterated part of the trail. It added some excitement to the trek, and by the time they reached their destination, everyone needed to use a flashlight to find footing.

"You folks go ahead and pitch your tents along here." Chet swung his arm in a line.

Della's brow puckered. "Why not over by the rocks? Wouldn't it be warmer there?"

"That's where we're having campfire."

"Oh." The minute Della dragged the tent to a spot, Misty and Madeline disappeared. The sisters didn't care to do much of anything. Their parents heaved sighs and raised their hands as if to say, "Oh, well," but Della noticed they didn't offer to help her pitch the tent. Once she had it up, she stored her gear inside.

Chet mentioned he had a permit for them to use deadwood and to have open fires. He and the other man scraped back a clear area, made a nominal ring of stones, and started the fire. They'd worked hard while folks pitched the tents to gather the wood and chop it to size, so Della dismissed the thought that the ring was too small. *They do this for a living. It's okay.*

Only it wasn't okay. Logs slid from the pyre, and one fell outside the perimeter stones. A few dried twigs and some grass caught fire, but folks stamped it out.

That wasn't the only problem. Chet arranged for everyone to sit against the rock wall and had the fire farther out, away from them. *Brandon taught me to build a fire close to the wall so the heat would radiate back and give double the heat. . . .*

A warm, hearty stew made from dehydrated stores bubbled on the fire and restored Della's faith in Rugged Adventures. They'd had no mishaps, and Chet showed fair navigation skills when they'd run into the need for a detour. *There's not just one way to do things. Brandon knew one way, but things are working all right this other way.*

Della snuggled into her sleeping bag and listened to the sisters complain about the hard ground and how cold they were. When she'd taken a closer look at their hip pads, she knew they had cause to grumble. *Brandon told me those were cheap. If it froze, they'd turn into sleds, and they didn't keep any cushion factor.* Only she couldn't share her pad — by design, they were only shoulder-to hip pieces. Even turning it sideways wouldn't help. The quality of the sleeping bags equaled the one he'd sneered at and left behind on their first camping trip.

By the next morning, Della drank the rest of her canteen and went to the creek to refill it. The other worker chuckled as she added water purification tablets.

"See how the water's running over all those rocks? That's nature's purifier. You don't need to use those pills."

"I thought the water had to rush over the stones and be white to be safe." *At least that's what Brandon said.*

"It's close enough."

Della hitched a shoulder. "Oh, well. Better safe than sorry." As soon as the words came out of her mouth, she bit her lip to keep from crying. Better safe than sorry . . . Brandon always said that when he took her camping.

SEVENTEEN

"I've got a bad feeling about Della's trip," Brandon said as he rolled up an electrical extension cord.

"Nothing you can do about it." Nathan looked out at the stakes in the bulldozed plot of earth that would become a housing development. "Put her in God's hands."

"I do. I have." Brandon dumped the bright orange, coiled cord onto a piece of plywood. "The problem is, I keep snatching her back. It's like I have her on a yo-yo string. She's God's . . . she's mine . . . she's God's. . . ."

"You don't know what she's learning. Could be, God's plan is going to unfold because of the things she finds out about herself on this trek. From what Jordan and Val tell me, when you went camping, you babied her."

"I most certainly did not. I showed her how to do things the right way."

Nathan shot him a telling look. "You made

the decisions. Her dad and brothers do the same thing to her. Maybe on this trip, when she has to do things for herself, she'll iron out some issues."

"Who says Della has issues?"

"Everyone has issues. You're having an issue right now — trying to make her out to be a saint when we both know she's a sinner. Just because you love someone and are loyal doesn't mean you view them as perfect."

"You could drive a man to violence," Brandon muttered.

"I'm trying to guide you to reason." Nathan unrolled the layout for the tract and weighted it down on the table. "I can't say Vanessa's helping, though. She insists that we need to have faith. We prayed last night, and we've decided to put a fleece before the Lord on your behalf."

"What's this fleece thing?"

"In the Old Testament. There was a mighty warrior, Gideon. He wanted to be sure of God's will, so he set a fleece on a threshing floor one night. If it was wet and the rest of the floor was dry, then he'd take it as God's will for him to go to battle."

"Well? Was the fleece wet?"

"Soaking. He squeezed out a whole bowlful of water."

Brandon nodded. "So he went to war."

"Nope. He decided to ask God for confirmation. The next night, the fleece was to be dry, and the rest of the floor was to become wet."

Brandon lifted a brow.

"Fleece was dry as a bone — the floor was wet."

"So Gideon sorta bugged God, too." For some reason, that thought pleased Brandon. He didn't feel quite so bad for having a hard time following the Lord's direction. "I'm gonna have to read more about that guy. Where is his story?"

"In the book of Judges."

"Okay. So what does that have to do with me?"

"Vanessa and I prayed over the tract. We walked it last night and felt led to a particular plot. If you select that plot, we're going to set it aside as a home for you and Della. We'll take it as His direction for your life. If you don't select it, I'm going to pray with you to let go of her completely."

Brandon stared at the horizon. "I already did that. The other night at the beach. I told God if she's not going to be His daughter, I wanted her to find someone else to love."

Nathan stayed quiet for a long while. Finally, he said, "That was part of it, but

191

not all of it. You asked God to have her let go of you. I don't hear you asking God to have you let go of her."

"I don't want to play this game."

"It's not a game. You decide. Van and I felt called, but we can't force you to do anything you don't want to. The offer's there. You decide."

Brandon wouldn't look down at the layout. He refused to.

Nathan quoted a line the SEALs used during training. "Sweat today or bleed tomorrow."

Ouch. That hit home like nothing else would. Brandon stared down at the paper. A decision like this ought to be made with a lot of forethought. Corner lots had bigger yards. Inside streets were quieter. In the past, when things were still good between him and Della, he'd secretly decided on just which place would be theirs. Fist tight, he passed it over the layout and fully intended to rap his knuckles on that segment, only his hand wouldn't go there. Instead, it veered to one side, and before he could figure out what he was doing, he'd decisively tapped a completely different lot.

"Number seventy-four." Nathan's voice sounded strained.

Brandon lifted his hand. "Don't say it."

"I have to. That's the one. It's the one Van and I consecrated last night to the Lord's will."

"Don't mess with my mind," Brandon rasped.

"I'm not. Here. Open this." Nathan took a small slip of paper from his pocket. "Van wrote a number on it."

Brandon's fingers shook as he unfolded it. There, in black and white was the number 74. "I'm not doing a second fleece. This is it." Brandon whooped. "She's mine!"

Things fell apart fast. After the second night, half of the hikers decided they'd had enough adventure. Cold and weary, sore-muscled and blister-footed, they couldn't imagine continuing into the rougher territory. The other guide led them back as Chet continued on with the rest of the group. Refusing to give up, Della stuck with those who would continue on.

"Babies," Chet muttered as they set out. "Soft. Why sign up for this if you want all the comforts of home? It's supposed to be something different."

"It's certainly been a challenge," Della said.

"Yeah. It's supposed to be." Chet looked pleased.

Della wasn't sure how he'd taken that as a compliment, but it didn't much matter. It wouldn't hurt for him to hear something nice after all of the complaints and criticism he'd heard over breakfast.

By late afternoon, Della's confidence in Chet's ability hit an all-time low. She felt sure she'd seen this stretch of the trail already today. They'd gone in a complete circle over the last hour. "How about if we look at the map?"

"Don't need to."

One of the other men stepped up beside her. "Don't growl at the girl. Seems to me, it was a reasonable request."

Della flashed him a smile of thanks.

"You can just GPS us," another hiker suggested.

"Battery went dead," Chet muttered.

A quick survey had them all on edge — only two of them had cellular phones, and neither was able to connect. Their batteries were incompatible with Chet's GPS.

They all crowded around the map. Brandon hadn't shown her how to read a map, but he'd taught her to gauge distance and direction. What the others decided made no sense to Della, but she held her tongue. Amongst them, they probably knew far more than she did about navigating.

"Okay. We'll need to set a good pace to reach the next site," Chet announced. "It'll probably be dark when we get there, but we managed just fine last night in the dark."

"We can do it," Della declared.

Two hours later, her confidence sank along with the sun. She'd refilled her canteen and followed Brandon's survival tips, but her feet and calves ached, and her back protested the weight of the backpack. Clouds started to roll in. Dusk turned to near dark, and still, they didn't stop.

"It's up here just a short ways. I know exactly where we are." Chet's declaration didn't inspire her as it did the others. Della stopped for a moment to rest then tagged along at the back of the line. One minute, her footing was solid. The next minute, her boot landed in empty space. The weight of her pack sent her careening over the edge and into darkness.

EIGHTEEN

Della groaned. Her leg hurt — not a little ache, but full-on, horrible pain. She couldn't even see it. About five feet away, a small circle of light let her know where her flashlight landed. She needed that light.

Gritting her teeth against the pain, she tried to stand. Impossible. Whimpers poured out of her as she worked her way to the flashlight. She stopped moving and caught her breath then yelled, "Hey! Somebody!"

No one answered.

Della figured they'd be back soon. In the meantime, she needed the flashlight. Once her hand curled around the plastic, she trained it on her knee to assess the damage.

Air shivered out of her lungs. Her jeans were shredded, and what she could see of her leg scared her. She laid back and talked to herself. "Stay calm. They'll come back. At least no bones are poking out. That's good."

Good? That opinion didn't last long. Within minutes, Della was cold. She shed her backpack and looked around. She couldn't have been unconscious for very long. Her party would be back for her in a few minutes, once they realized she was missing.

In the meantime, she needed to take care of herself. She had nothing to wrap her knee except her bandana. It would suffice for now. Surely, Chet carried an Ace bandage. Gritting her teeth, she poured water over the scraped mess and bound her knee as best she could. "Hey guys! I'm stuck over here. I could use some help."

Her voice shook with cold and pain. Tugging on her backpack, she shifted it so she could pull out a hooded sweat shirt.

One thing at a time. Think ahead. Plan. Brandon's words kept streaming through her mind. They kept her from panicking. Della couldn't find the whistle she'd brought along. Brandon made everyone in their party wear a lanyard with a whistle in case they got lost. *Just pucker up your lips and give me a whistle. I'll come running, Babe.*

"Oh, Brandon. Why can't you come get me now?" She raised her voice, "I'm hurt, guys. C'mon and find me, will you?"

Only she heard no one.

The place she'd landed had plenty of sticks and branches — but that was about as stupid of a place as possible for her to stay. She wouldn't be spotted, and the danger of snakes . . . she cut off that line of thought. Della searched her surroundings and decided on where to go.

Hug a tree. You get lost; you hug a tree. People wander all over and can't be found because they don't stay put.

A tree about eight feet away looked like a good spot. She scrabbled toward it one painful inch at a time. About a yard from her goal, she felt something hit her hand. Then her face.

Rain.

Sobbing, Della pulled herself the last few feet and slumped against the tree. "Why, God? What did I do that's so bad? Why are You punishing me?"

Slowly, she opened her eyes. Daylight. Surely they'd come looking and find her. They couldn't be far away. Della groaned as she unwound the extra-large trash bag from around herself. It kept her warm and fairly dry last night — another one of Brandon's little helpful hints. She popped two aspirin and washed them down with a big gulp of water. *How did that commercial go? Take two aspirin and call me in the morning.*

"Me! Oh, me — eeee!" she shouted. "I took the aspirin. I did my part. Now come help me!"

No one answered.

After a few hours, Della's hopes began to flag. At first, she'd thought maybe Chet and the others had a little trouble. Then she thought they couldn't very well look for her during last night's rain. But they should have come back by now.

A galling fact glared at her: Chet couldn't punch his way out of a plastic garbage bag. *He has no right to run a business when he doesn't know anything. They've left me here. What am I going to do?*

As if she didn't know what she'd packed, Della emptied her backpack entirely. Taking stock of her supplies now took on a whole new significance. The big bag of Brandon's favorite beef jerky looked better than anything she'd ever eaten. A container of trail mix, two candy bars, a fruit leather, and a package of gum. Not a promising supply, but adequate for a day or two if she paced herself.

Water, though. A slosh let her know her canteen stood about half-full. She'd need more water — soon. By midday, thirst and the understanding that no one was searching for her forced Della to decide to find a water source. Using a stick as a cane, she jump-hopped her way around. Each move sent spears of agony through her.

She lost track of time. Lost track of where she was. Cried. Finally, Della found a creek. She sat down in the water and let the coolness surround her swollen knee. After drinking the last sip from her canteen, she refilled it. Then she wondered if she ought to skip using the purification tablets. One man said yes; the other said no. *Who do I trust?*

She added the tablets.

At first, getting wet felt good. Clean. Bracing and refreshing and helped lessen the pain. But then reality sank in. Her jeans wouldn't dry before sunset. She couldn't light a fire to signal for help or to use for heat. Though she had a lighter, she couldn't collect enough wood to do the job and still set up a safe fire ring. The last thing she wanted to do was start a forest fire and be its first fatality.

"Water. Warmth. Food." She kept chanting the priorities. Della wished she'd been carrying a tent now. Her sleeping bag and garbage bag would have to suffice. Gnawing on a piece of beef jerky, she studied her surroundings. She needed a big, solid, friendly-looking tree. Then she'd get there, change her clothes, and wait.

Someone would search for her. Brandon would.

Only she'd told him to leave her alone.

"He left her alone up there?" Brandon's bellow nearly shook the construction trailer.

"Yes," Della's father answered in an anguished tone. He shoved his hands in his pockets. "Listen. We told you to leave her be, but I'm asking —"

"I'm going after her."

"Good."

Having been in the military set habits that he'd not broken yet. Brandon always kept a pack ready so he could roll out the minute he got a call. His pack sat at the ready in the bottom of his closet at home. As he went to claim it, he dialed Lurch. If the guys were on maneuvers, that was that — but if they were home, Brandon couldn't come up with a better team of men to help him get his woman.

Lurch's phone kept ringing. No help from that quarter.

Soon as he hung up, Nathan called. "I'm coming along. Jim Martinez, too."

"I'm heading out now."

"Pick me up at Jim's."

"No way. I'm not wasting a minute."

"We're on the way, Brandon."

"Be out front. If you're not, I won't stop."

Nathan and Jim stood on the curb. Katie and Van were there, too, with a crate and a duffel bag of junk. Brandon itched to gun the engine, and the women were gabbing about food and clothes and stupid inconsequentials.

"Later," he rumbled. "She's been out there alone for two nights already. We can't waste time."

"God go with you!" Van called.

Brandon pulled out into traffic and growled, "The guys are out on maneuvers. We're on short team."

Nathan grinned at him like a madman. "Did I ever tell you about a guy named Gideon?"

"Yeah. Him and the fleece."

"There's another story about him. He had a big army, but God only let him take the warriors who drank from their hands instead of burying their face in the water."

"Let me guess. His side still won."

"God always wins." Nathan smacked the dashboard. "You can count on that."

"Let's see . . ." Della spoke aloud to herself all of the time now. She didn't care if it was odd. It gave her a little comfort. "What next?"

She'd calculated things as best she could. Chet would have spent time searching for her, but because of the rain, he wouldn't have much luck with tracks. Sad truth was, even if it hadn't rained, Della seriously doubted he would have been able to trace her footprints back to where she'd fallen, let alone to where she'd wandered from there to the creek. After a nominal effort, Chet would give up then head back with the others. Even at a full run, that meant they'd still have a day and a half to hike out; then help would take another day or two to come here. From that point, they'd have to look all over the forest to find her. Five days. Yes, five. That sounded about right.

But the pain in her knee said she couldn't wait for help that long.

Della counted out how many aspirin she had and rationed them to last five days. She did the same with her food. By dumping the trail mix into the pocket of her sweat shirt, she was able to use that pint-sized container to hold more water.

She'd hacked off her blue jeans and cut off the leg at thigh-level of the other pair before she pulled them on. Every move sent shards of pain through her.

Don't tense. Don't fight the pain. Let it be there. Brandon's words to her as he'd rubbed out a nasty charley horse she'd gotten during a morning beach run echoed in her mind. *Blow like you're blowing away the pain.*

She'd practically hyperventilated when she changed her clothes, but she got it done. Brandon was right — it worked. Sort of. Not that all the pain disappeared, but she'd coped.

He was right about the tent stakes and gauging distance and . . . She stopped cold. "What if he's right about God?"

"No. It's not like that," she answered herself. "I'm going to stay busy. I don't have to think about God and Jesus and all that religion stuff."

Lying on the hip pad with her head pillowed on a wadded up sleeping bag nearly drove her crazy. Thoughts of Brandon swirled around in her head. "I'm thinking of him because I'm in the wilderness. It's just mental association. What I need to do is stay busy." She sat up and pulled over her backpack. With all the supplies she stuffed in there, she could rig up some kind of a tent between the two shrubs with her garbage bag.

■ ■ ■ ■

The others started to turn in for the night. They'd put in half of yesterday and all of today searching for Della, but to no avail. Chet couldn't be specific about where he'd led his party that last night, let alone where he'd lost Della. Thick vegetation made it impossible for helicopters to give much assistance. Thermal imaging should help, but to Brandon's frustration, it hadn't yielded anything useful. Search dogs hadn't picked up her scent either.

"Rest up. We'll start first thing in the morning," Nathan urged.

Brandon shook his head then dug through his gear and pulled out night vision goggles. "I'm heading out north by northwest."

"Alone?" Jim gawked at him. "We don't need another —"

Brandon's glower silenced him. He bent, snagged his pack, and shrugged into it. "Grab me more water, will you?"

Jim trotted off, and Nathan offered, "I'll come with you."

"No can do. My NVGs will keep me from breaking my neck. Thanks, but no thanks." He accepted the bottles Jim brought back, stuffed two into the pockets of his pack, and glugged down the third. He shoved the empty bottle back into Nathan's hand. "Wanna know something weird? I was just reading about the shepherd leaving the flock to search for that one lost lamb."

His boss grinned. "And we all know He succeeds. God go with you."

Brandon set off at a steady pace and yanked on the NVGs. The band pulled at his hair — something it never did when he sported a near buzz cut. The greenish glow from the lenses felt good. Familiar. He was on a mission, and this one — it had to be successful.

'Round about midnight, Brandon came upon a spot that showed excessive trampling. His pulse rose. The fire ring and divots in the ground showed a group camped here overnight very recently. At least now the search field could be focused. According to his GPS, they were miles off course — a massive distance in this terrain.

"What would you do, Della?" he muttered as he unfolded a detailed satellite map of the area and flipped up the NVGs. The green tint on this map made it difficult to read. Training his flashlight on it, he looked for a water source. If she followed all of his teaching, she would have hugged a tree, but thirst would drive her toward water after a day.

There. A small stream. It meandered off toward the east. He would locate it then search the full length along both sides. After taking a fix on his location, he set out. It didn't take long before he heard the subtle trickling of water flow. Pine and fir trees blocked any distance vision.

Ten thousand feet altitude. The temperature dipped to the low 40s. Brandon hoped Della brought the sleeping bag he'd selected for her instead of renting one of the cheap jobs Chet used. She had to be hungry. Hypothermia was all she needed. Poor woman had to be scared out of her mind.

God, lead me to her. Help me find her. Let her be okay.

Brandon tamped down his fears. That fleece thing — that meant he and Della had a future together. She'd make it through this. Once he got her out of here, though, he'd never let go of her.

Methodically using trees as points of reference, Brandon searched both sides of the creek. No human footprints joined those of raccoons, mule deer, and coyotes. No signs of human habitation — no footprints or drag-and-scrap lines showed anyone had been here. Brandon knew he might miss signs that would stand out in daylight — a scrap of cloth, a food wrapper. *I have to have faith. God will lead me.*

Coyotes howled. Crickets sang. Water bubbled. Wind soughed. He strained to detect anything out of the ordinary. By now, even if she'd rationed use of the flashlight, her batteries would be toast. Della, huddled alone in the dark — cold, hungry, and scared. The thought made him sick. He forged on.

Lord, I'm seeing a new side of Your love — of how You relentlessly pushed on and pursued me. Only I didn't even know I was lost, so I kept marching farther and farther away. This time, it's You and me together — looking for Della — both body and soul. I want it all, God. I want her in my arms. I want You in her heart. . . .

Then he saw it: a stack of rocks in the center of the narrow creek. They'd been carefully arranged from large to small to form a stack several inches high — something that wouldn't have happened in nature. She'd left him a signal! Plowing ahead, Brandon sloshed through the icy water and stared at that stack then scanned banks. One bore deep grooves and left-sided footprints. *Della's hurt. But she's nearby!*

"Della!" he shouted as he headed up the

bank and followed the marked earth. His goggles illuminated a lump. Della. Only she didn't move or make a sound.

Nineteen

"Della!"

She jarred awake to something crashing into her makeshift shelter. Della screamed then shrieked even louder when she saw the monster. Clutching her flashlight, she clobbered him.

"Hey! Della!"

She froze.

"Babe —"

"Brandon!" She dropped the flashlight and grabbed for him, trying to assure herself she hadn't gone crazy. He was here. Holding her. "You came. It's really you."

"You bet it is."

"What are you wearing?"

He yanked off the weird lenses and blinked. "Night vision goggles." He pressed her back down.

"You scared me half silly." She lay back and stared up at him as he pressed fingers to the side of her neck. "My pulse is about

210

three hundred from that scare."

"I noticed." His tone held wry humor. He proceeded to take stock of her.

"If you dare touch my leg, I'm going to start banging you with the flashlight again."

"Which leg?"

"Right."

Brandon sat back on his heels and shed his pack. It made a loud thump on the earth, and Della wondered just how much gear he'd been toting. He'd done it for her. What did that mean, though?

"Shhh, Babe. Don't cry. It'll be all right." He leaned over her and rubbed his whiskery jaw against her cheek.

Della hadn't realized she'd started to cry. The sandpapery feel of his jaw testified to his masculinity, to the fact that he was here — strong and capable. She didn't have to be strong anymore. Until now, she'd convinced herself to be courageous, but the strain of it finally took its toll. Once the tears started to fall, she couldn't stop them.

Cupping her hand over her mouth, she tried to tamp back the sobs. Brandon had come for her — but only as a friend. They'd never been closer, but they'd never been further apart.

Grim determination painted his features and colored his voice. "I'm going to take a look at your leg."

If he wanted to think pain prompted this reaction, Della decided that would be okay. At least it would help her save face later. Being offered nothing more than friendship by the man she loved caused her far more pain than her hurt leg.

He rested his forehead against hers. His warm breath whispered across her face. "You lie still."

She wanted him to kiss her, to promise everything would be okay, but he didn't. He pulled away and passed his flashlight up and down over her until he figured out how she'd wrapped herself in the sleeping bag. The man was all business. Methodical. Careful. Swift.

The cold night air hit her, but he quickly tucked the sleeping bag back around all but her right leg. He blew on his hands, rubbed them together for a second to warm them, then began at her ankle.

She'd started to regain a little composure. Della wiped away her tears and rasped, "It's my knee."

"Okay." He ignored her and continued to examine her from ankle upward prodding at her with all the compassion of a Sherman tank. Then he started to unknot the bandana she'd tied around her knee.

"Aaghh — no — no — no!" She'd bolted into a sitting position without realizing it. Waves of pain caused her to hit his hands away.

"All right, Babe. It's all right." He held her by the shoulders and eased her to lie back down again. Tugging the sleeping bag back up to warm her, he grated, "I'm sorry. It's real sore. I know."

"Don't —"

"I'm not going to touch your knee. I'm checking above it."

The next several minutes turned into a blur of agony. She heard his voice, but whatever he said didn't make any sense. All Della wanted was for him to stop. Finally, he scooted upward and cupped her cheeks.

"I've immobilized it. I can't tell whether you've just wrenched it, cracked the knee-cap, or torn ligaments. It's too swollen to guess. The pulses are strong — that's a good thing, Babe. Really good."

Through her tear-glazed vision, in the muted beam of the flashlight, his remorse came through. Della bit the inside of her cheek and nodded.

Nothing escaped him. His lips thinned. "I don't have anything to give you for pain."

"I'm okay if I stay warm and don't move."

"Come morning, I'll signal for help. I can

carry you to a clearing not far from here, and we'll airlift you out." His eyes narrowed. "You're starting to shiver."

The man wouldn't give up. He ripped open a foil-like survival blanket and tore back her sleeping bag.

"Brandon!"

"You'll build up heat again in a sec." He spread the survival blanket over her, tucked the sleeping bag around her shoulders again, and then brushed strands of hair away from her face.

She gave him her bravest smile. "It's not so bad now."

A smile chased across his face, but he remained intense. "Hungry? Thirsty?"

"I was going to ask you the same thing. My canteen's about a third full, and I still have a piece of jerky left."

"You brought jerky?"

She nodded. No use reminding him of how he taught her to bring high protein, lightweight food. That was all over . . . in the past.

"How about some cocoa?"

"I don't have any."

His chuckle sounded rough. "I didn't expect you to have anything at all left to eat or drink. I've got rations in my pack — even cocoa."

"Oh, that sounds good."

A can of Sterno, and the man turned into a gourmet. The unmistakable aroma of cocoa filled the night air. He held up her head and shoulders and poured a cup of the rich, warm drink down her throat. "Better?"

"The best."

She watched as he looked around and tied up the fishing line he'd broken when he ripped down her shelter. She'd knotted fishing line to her towel and strung it between shrubs then tied the torn-open trash bag over it. Crumpled pages from a book and pine needles stuffed between the towel and bag acted as insulation to help keep her cooler during the day and warmer at night — a trick he'd told her about. Approval colored his voice. "You did a good job establishing a base camp."

"I had a great teacher." She looked at him. "When I got going on this trip and Chet did things differently, I thought there were probably other ways to do the chores; but everything went wrong. Some things, there's just one right way, isn't there?"

"Yeah." He studied her at length. "Are you just talking about camping?"

"No." She sighed. "I had a mother bring in the flower girl a few days ago. Because her daughter is a redhead, she didn't ever dress her in pink because she'd gotten the notion that it wouldn't look right. By the time she left, she said the truth was in front of her, but she'd refused to see it."

Brandon didn't say a thing.

Della closed her eyes. "What if I've been wrong? What if you're right? That there's only one right way to live? That I'm not good enough for God? I've been lying here for days now, and I can't get away from it. I figured it out. You couldn't compromise because we couldn't be a team with both of us going off in different directions. But I didn't want to change for you."

"It's not a decision you make based on someone else. You have to do it for yourself."

She nodded. "I figured that out, too."

He started making more cocoa. Deft, purposeful movements, and silence reigned. "Here."

"No, Brandon. You drink that one. In fact, you need to get in your sleeping bag, too. It's cold out tonight — colder than the other nights."

She tried to scoot closer to him, but the effort hurt.

"Hang on, Babe." He opened his own sleeping bag and draped it around her. "Better?"

216

"I'm warm enough."

"Ahhh." Brandon sat cross-legged and reached under the sleeping bags to hold her hand. "So what have you been thinking?"

"All my life, I've tried to be good enough — to be what Daddy and my brothers wanted me to be. To please teachers and customers and, well, to be perfect. Not that I ever managed all of those things, but I tried. Then I met you, and you showed me I didn't have to do anything to make you like me — you just took me as I was. You gave me a chance to try stuff and encouraged me even when I was lousy at batting or running or camping. For you, I didn't have to be perfect. I was good enough — just me."

She couldn't stop the flow of words once she started. "Then, suddenly, you told me I wasn't perfect. I had to change. If I didn't change, I wasn't good enough for you anymore."

He looked like he wanted to say something, but Della was afraid if she let him, she'd lose her nerve.

"But I've been lying here thinking. God doesn't expect me to be perfect, does He? To Him, I'm already a disaster. All the things I've done wrong, all that stuff — He already knows it. The bottom line is, He'll still take me, right?"

"God loves you, Della. He knows everything about you, and it breaks His heart to have the distance sin created between you. He gave His Son just so you could be forgiven."

"So what you're saying is, I blew it a thousand million billion times, and He still wants me."

"Yeah."

"But what do I have to give Him for that? Jesus died for my sins, and I can't do anything to repay my debt."

"The debt's been cancelled — but you have to accept that fact. The cost is that you have to be sold out to God. You get a new life — a different life. I still blow it, but He forgives me, and I try to do better."

"What about all the rules and stuff?"

"I always thought there were a lot of rules for Christians. Now that I am one, I'm discovering there really aren't many. I'm to live in obedience to the Bible and to the directions I feel God leads me. The Golden Rule and the Ten Commandments pretty much cover it all" — he paused — "except for what happened between us."

Tears slipped down her cheeks. "You were right though. If we'd gotten married, I wouldn't have stayed happy. In my heart of hearts, I'd sense you wanted more from me, that I disappointed you."

His shoulders slumped. "I'm glad you understand that. It nearly killed me, hurting you like that."

"It's torn me apart."

TWENTY

Brandon didn't say a word. He didn't need to. Agony pulled his features taut.

Della winced as she reached to reassure him. "I never want to live through that kind of pain again. At first, I blamed you. I blamed God. Then I had to admit that I made a choice."

He sat so still, so somber. Della wasn't sure he understood what she was saying, but she strove to order her thoughts so they'd make sense.

"I decided, being stuck out here with nothing to do but think, that I'm like that little redhead's mom — the truth was right in front of me, but I hadn't accepted it. I just don't know what I'm supposed to do."

"Della, are you saying to want to commit your life to Christ?"

She nodded.

"It's not just so you and I —"

"No." She squeezed his hand. "I couldn't

live a lie."

"Oh, Babe, I prayed so hard for you to open your heart to Jesus."

"What do I do?"

"We pray. You confess to God that you've sinned and know Jesus is the price to rescue you from sin. You ask Him into your heart. It's that simple."

"I can't figure out why He wants me, but I'm glad He does."

"It's a special kind of love — a love worth finding. We have to search our souls and make the decision, but I promise you, Della, you won't be sorry."

"Well, here goes everything." She laid her head back, switched off the flashlight, and stared up at the stars. "I like the idea of looking up at the heavens to say my first prayer."

Brandon rubbed his thumb across her palm in agreement.

"Dear God, it's me. Della. Oh. You know that. You know everything. Then You know what I'm doing here. I've tried to live right, but I blow it. I can't do it on my own, and there's no way I can earn my way into heaven. I'm offering a trade here — my old life for a new one. You'll have to work on me with this new life, because I'm bound to mess up on things. But I'll do my best to

221

follow what You ask of me. I'll even go to church and read the Bible and all that stuff because — well, not because it's a rule, but because I'm grateful and love You. Amen."

"I've never heard sweeter words in my whole life, Babe."

She wasn't hypothermic or dehydrated, and though her knee hurt, the circulation to her lower leg was fine. Brandon knew he didn't need to transport her out tonight. If he did, he'd have to carry her several miles — something he wouldn't mind in the least. He had hold of her and wasn't about to ever let go. Though a new Christian, he knew the gift God had bestowed upon him tonight was a rare and precious thing. A man couldn't want more than the woman he loved to find the Lord. But trekking out would pose too much of a strain on Della. The terrain was too uneven, and though he'd take every precaution to plot out the smoothest course and carry her with every scrap of devotion he felt, she wouldn't be able to endure much jarring. If he waited until morning, he'd be able to carry her to a nearby clearing, signal, and airlift her smoothly.

The strength of the pulses in her foot and ankle gave much-needed reassurance, because from just above the knee down, she was a bruised, battered wreck. Trying to get the cocoa into her made sense — warm fluids, sugar — they'd help in case she was shocky. Only she wasn't. Despite her pain, she stayed uncannily calm. His woman had gumption.

Brandon flicked on the flashlight. "Babe, about getting you out of here . . ."

She shook her head and yawned. "I'm glad you said we'd wait 'til tomorrow. I don't want to be a sissy or anything, but my leg hurts a lot more at night when it's cold."

"No one in his right mind would call you a sissy. You're a gutsy woman. I'm proud of you."

She squeezed his hand. "You've got to be getting cold, and I'm roasting under two of these sleeping bags."

"Hang on a few minutes." He took the small pan of water he'd left over the Sterno and soaked it up with a pair of Handi Wipes. "Wash up. You'll relax and sleep better."

She started scrubbing at her face. "Do I look that bad?"

"You're the most beautiful woman in the world."

"I haven't," she asserted as she washed her jaw and throat, "shampooed my hair in a week. I'm filthy."

"To God, you're pure as snow. To me, you're lovely."

"You're nice to say those things. Really, you are. But I feel atrocious." She whisked the cloth over her forearms and hands, then grimaced at how dirty the wipe had become. Brandon silently took it and gave her the other one. Just like a fastidious kitten, she set about washing her face again. "I ran out of my sun block lotion two days ago, and vain as it sounds, I really didn't want anymore freckles."

"I'm wild about your freckles. They make me want to kiss you silly."

"So what are you waiting for?"

Brandon leaned forward then pulled back. "Sweetheart, I love you. Before I found Jesus, I knew you were the woman I wanted for my wife — and I gotta tell you, I've had a ring about burning a hole in my pocket . . . because I had to have faith that you'd find your way to the Lord. His love is worth finding, Della. I want my love for you to be worth it, too. Will you marry me?"

"Oh, yes. Please, yes! I love you so much, Brandon."

He leaned to one side and yanked his wallet from his back pocket. Inside nested the ring he'd chosen for her. "I'm putting this on your finger and allowing myself one last kiss." He smiled. "But then, no kisses until the wedding. Otherwise, I'm afraid you're going to dally for months planning an extravaganza, and I don't want to wait anymore. All I want is you and me, blessed by God, being husband and wife."

The ring fit just right. Their lips fit just right, too. A kiss never held so much promise and love. Brandon finally pulled away, crawled into his sleeping bag, and had her use his chest as a pillow. She settled in with a sigh.

"Brandon?"

"Yeah, Babe?"

"I already know what tux I want you to wear."

"Good."

"And I already know my favorite music. Do you have any songs you like a lot?"

"I'm not picky. But I do want you to carry white flowers. Roses."

"Could we compromise? Valentine brides always carry red roses."

"By compromise, do you mean you'll carry pink ones, or a combination of red and white?" He chuckled. Of all the times he'd lain out under the stars, most had been consumed with the tension of a mission. He'd never imagined he'd spend time worrying about the color of flowers.

"Either."

"Red and white," he decided. "I'll talk Nathan into letting us have a reception at The Spindles. How does that sound?"

"I'd love that!"

"Great. So all the big decisions are made. We can get this done soon."

"My gown —"

He groaned. "Oh, no. Linda's mom said it took five months for her gown. You can't do that to me. I'll go insane."

"She wanted a special Belgian lace that was on back order."

"No Belgian lace." He tapped her shoulder to make sure she heard him.

"I love Belgian lace."

He sighed. Once upon a time, he'd decided to give her time to whip up the wedding of her dreams. Right about now, he'd gladly have her dad wheel her down the aisle in a wheelchair with her dressed in a coonskin cap and swimsuit.

Her cheek rubbed his shirtfront as she looked up at him. "Really, no Belgian lace?" She sounded so disappointed. But lace was so . . . impossibly trivial.

"Belgian is for waffles, not lace."

"Oh." She sighed. "I didn't know you felt that way. Next thing you're going to say is Brussels is out because of sprouts. French is

226

out because of toast."

"And fries," he added. "What is this, anyway? Who goes around naming frilly stuff after European countries?"

"The people who've perfected the art of creating beautiful lace."

He groaned. "Just how long is this Belgian lace going to take?"

Her shoulders began to shake, and her voice filled with laughter. "The gown I love with Belgian lace is at my shop right now."

"Hot dog!"

"You're making me hungry."

"You're making me crazy. Go to sleep."

"Mornin' beautiful."

"Hi." She hitched up on both elbows. "You're up early."

"I got a signal out. You're due for a ride in about half an hour."

"Half an hour?" She sat up and groaned at how the action pulled her leg.

Brandon nodded then wondered as she rummaged in her backpack, "What're you looking for?"

"My brush. Ouch! Found it!" She looked at him pleadingly. "Can you take me to the creek and help me dunk my head? I have shampoo."

He frowned.

"It's biodegradable. It won't hurt the environment or ecosystem or anything."

"Honey, it's going to take me twenty minutes to get you to the extraction point."

"Then we don't have time to waste!"

"The water's cold."

"Refreshing," she shot back.

He heaved a sigh. "Vanity, thy name is woman."

Della gave him a sassy smile. "I'm a Christian now. Cleanliness is next to godliness."

It took a little fancy maneuvering, but Brandon humored her. After laying her on his trash bag, he used the small pan to help rinse out the shampoo then tackled one side of her hair with his comb as she used her brush on the other. While she braided it, he packed up their sleeping bags, took the gear out of her backpack and stowed it in his then used the frame to rig a splint for her leg.

Della reached over and threaded her fingers through his hair as he used the cording to tie the last knot. "You're an incredible man. You know how to do so much."

"I'd better warn you; I can't cook."

"So what? I love to cook. You know that."

"Then we're definitely a match made in heaven, because I've eaten your food." He tugged on his pack. It looked impossibly heavy. Della marveled at his strength.

Then he scooped her up.

"Brandon!"

"Put your arm around my neck. I know it's hard on you —"

"Hard on me! Do you know how much I weigh — no, don't answer that."

"I've carried ugly old rafts that weigh more than you." He set off walking.

"If you get me a stick, I can hobble."

He snorted — a purely masculine sound that dismissed her offer without bothering to even entertain it for a moment. He acted as if this were his own backyard — picking his path with the absolute assurance of where he was going, twisting to the side to avoid banging her leg on trees and bushes.

"Brandon, how did you signal?"

"Mirror."

"No kidding? I thought you'd have some super-spy satellite thingamabob. You mean I could have just used my compact?"

"The mountains make signals bounce. Electronic gear's unreliable out here. As for the mirror — you were under a canopy of trees. Not enough room to refract back up. Besides, I'd guess you don't know Morse code."

"It's on the inside cover of my survival book, but the directions don't tell how to make a dot or a dash."

Her leg burned. Even though he did everything humanly possible to ease her way, Della hurt. He distracted her as best he could with tidbits of information and idle conversation. It was so unlike him just to chat about nothing — but he did it for her.

It made Della love him that much more.

They reached a clearing, and he laid her down in a small, grassy patch then consulted his watch. "We made good time."

"Even with washing my hair." She smiled at him. "Did I thank you for that?"

"Only a hundred times or so."

She looked down at herself. "Now I understand why the military uses those grays and khakis. They don't show the dirt. I'm covered in grunge."

"It's about to get worse." His voice rang with unrepentant glee.

"Why?"

"Chopper backwash."

Once the helicopter arrived, everything happened quickly. A basket came down, and Brandon lifted her into it, strapped, buckled, and stood.

Fear suddenly swamped her. She'd be hanging in this basket by a mere rope! *God, I know it's awful early for me to be asking things of You, but I'm so scared. Please help me.*

Brandon writhed in a few blurring motions then took a hook and clipped it to the rope. "Ready for the ride of your life?"

"With you?" Her heart stopped thundering. God answered her prayer more quickly and much better than she could have imagined.

"Yeah." He gave a signal, and they lifted off.

Once inside the helicopter, Brandon scooted off to one side. Medics converged around her, asking questions and yanking back the covers.

In one slim minute she had an IV and felt like she'd been caught in a spider web of electronic wires. Brandon leaned forward and barked, "Give her something. She hurts."

They radioed, took an order, and pulled a syringe out of a package. Brandon leaned close and hollered in her ear, "You're okay now, Babe. You'll feel lots better in just a second."

She tried her hardest to smile at him, but the world started to tilt crazily then spin. Reaching toward him to grab his hand, she cried, "Bra—" but the world went dark.

TWENTY-ONE

"We need permission to treat. Who's the next of kin?"

Brandon dumped Della's bag on the floor of the Emergency Department. "She has an emergency treatment consent card signed in her wallet. Do what you need to."

When they'd gone camping, she'd laughed at his attention to that seemingly ridiculous detail and proclaimed she trusted him to keep her safe. He'd insisted; now he was glad he had.

"I want to go back to be with her."

"Are you family?"

"We're engaged." Happy words, those.

"I guess it's okay. She's in bay three."

Brandon strode back and stood outside the curtains. "Permission to enter?"

Someone chuckled. "Permission granted."

"Thanks." He parted the curtains and stepped inside. Dressed in one of those ridiculous hospital gowns, Della lay on the gurney fast asleep. It did his heart good to see the deeply etched lines of pain gone from around her eyes and lips. "How is she?"

"Minimal exposure. She did a great job of staying hydrated and warm. We're taking her to X-ray her leg."

"Thanks." While they took her off, he ducked into the men's room, splashed off, and shaved. As he swiped off the last swatch of his day-old stubble, he had to laugh. "Who would have ever guessed that I'd become this domesticated?"

It hurt to raise his arms to peel off his shirt. Between sleeplessness, sleeping on the hard ground, and carrying two packs and Della at the same time, his shoulder took considerable strain. He'd pay for it, but the cost was negligible; the joy he'd gained from leading Della to the Lord and asking her to become his wife were priceless. Eternal. He yanked on a clean T-shirt, grinned at his reflection, and headed back to sit by Della in the treatment room.

Wheels and rubber-soled shoes squeaked on the linoleum floor, and Della's gurney slid back into the bay. He squinted at the nurse's badge. "Mary Jo. What did the X-rays show?"

"Doc will talk with you." She pointed to a

jumble of lightweight aluminum tubes on the floor. "That was an ingenious splint."

"If you have a bag, I'll haul it out of here."

"How long was she lost?"

A lifetime. "Five days.

"Hurt, scared, and alone. Poor girl."

"She'll recover. She'll be better than ever."

"That's the spirit." Mary Jo took another pasty-colored flannel blanket out of a steel cabinet. "These are warmed. Ought to feel good to her."

"Thanks." Brandon helped her spread it over Della and noted how the nurse took care to leave Della's knee exposed, yet tucked the blankets back around her foot so she'd be warm enough. The ER was drafty.

"If I didn't know better, I would have thought she took a spill off a cycle." Mary Jo tucked towels under Della's leg and started cleaning it with Betadine. "She's got quite a road rash down the side of this leg. It's amazing it's not infected."

"She told me she poured hand sanitizer on it."

"Oh, *ow*. That had to hurt. Those are alcohol based."

The doctor came back in and shoved three X-rays onto a light box. "She's got a hairline fracture at the head of the tibia. Patella's not cracked. We had an MRI cancellation, so I want to slip her in that slot and see if she tore any ligaments."

"Great!"

The doctor gave him a dark look.

Brandon shrugged. "I believe in miracles. God let that machine be available for my Della."

"I see," the doctor said, but Brandon could tell by his tone he didn't see at all. What a pity.

"Her ring — she can't have on any metal in the machine." Mary Jo tugged off Della's engagement ring. "How about if you hold this for her?"

"Yeah."

An hour and a half later, the doctor shook his head. "Someone's guardian angel was watching out for her. The preliminary reading by our radiologist says the ligaments are okay. The swelling's from the fracture and blood in the joint. She's too swollen to cast, but I can tap her knee."

"Do it," Brandon decided aloud as he slipped the ring back on her finger. He smiled at Mary Jo. "Let's not tell her that came off. She's sentimental."

Della hobbled across her shop on the fiberglass walking cast. "Brandon!"

"What are you doing here?" He scowled.

"You need to be taking it easy."

"I got my cast last night. See?"

He looked down and burst out laughing.

"I thought it looked spectacular."

"Who did that?"

She glanced past the hem of her pale blue-and-white floral sundress at the pale pink fiberglass affair that went from her toes to just above her knee. "Vanessa glued on the pearls and silver beads. Valene painted the designs and lettering."

Ellen Zobel straightened a gown on a nearby mannequin. "I wish I had my daughters' artistic talent. I can't get this right."

"Once you accessorize it with the necklace and bouquet, it'll look perfect." Without Ellen's help, Della would have had to close down the shop. She'd been, literally, a godsend.

Brandon ignored their exchange and stayed focused on Della's cast. He read aloud, "Here comes the bride," then tilted his head to study the hearts and curlicues. "It's great. Especially the top. Who did that?"

She didn't dare look down again and played coy. "Oh, that little thing?"

He nodded. "I like the blue ribbon on it."

"Well, you know the old saying, something old, something new, something borrowed, something blue, and" — she wiggled to give him a side view of her foot where they'd glued one last item — "a penny in her shoe."

He threw back his head and belted out a deep, wonderful laugh.

Della slipped her arms around his waist — as much for balance as affection, and he held her. "I'm one of a kind, Brandon."

"Babe, I'm so glad I found you!" He shifted her to the side, stooped, and swept her off her feet. Striding toward a padded bench over by the dressing rooms, he tacked on, "But I'm not happy at all about you zipping around. I want you to heal" — his voice dropped to a thrillingly deep, low level — "fast."

Della rested her head on his shoulder. "Doc said four weeks."

Brandon growled.

She laughed. "That's barely enough time to order, receive, and send out the invitations."

"You're on your own there. You've seen my handwriting." He seated her on the bench and tickled her newly painted toes.

"It would help if you gave me a guest list."

Ellen groaned aloud. "You don't know what you're asking for. When Val married Jordan, he invited hundreds of guys he'd known in the service."

"That's fine with me." Della beamed up at Brandon. "This is the happiest day of my life. Everyone's welcome to share it!"

"How many does the church hold?" Brandon gave her a calculating look.

"Five hundred." Demurely tugging down the hem of her dress, she added, "I did a layout of The Spindles and figured if we use the entire downstairs, we can seat four hundred and twenty-five for a meal."

He whistled. "That's gonna be steep."

"Nope." Della gave him a perky smile. "One of the benefits of my business — the caterer, musicians, photographer, and Forget Me Not Flowers all offered to do everything at cost."

"Great." Brandon clapped his hands together and rubbed them. "I've got a bunch of men who'll never go to church, but they'll come to my wedding — especially if I tell them you've invited single friends."

"Okay. I know a lot of single women. We can have Pastor MacIntosh do what he did at your cousin's wedding — give the salvation message."

"One other important thing." Brandon tilted her face upward. "No negotiating. I want you to promise me you won't wear heels."

"You, too? What is this?" Della let out a sigh. "Daddy, the doctor, my brothers, Van and Val — everyone is nagging me about that."

"Ellen? Did she listen to them?"

Ellen bustled over and showed him a pair of beaded satin ballet-type slippers. "I chose these for her. What do you think?"

He took one and shoved his thumbs inside then pulled on it. "It stretches. If it were a little bigger, it would fit over the cast. . . ."

"You're nuts!" Della cried.

"Yep. Certifiably crazy about you." He set the slipper onto the bench beside her and straightened up. "We're pouring the foundation of our house this afternoon. Wanna come watch?"

"Yes!" She hopped up from the bench and hobbled toward the cash register.

"What are you doing?"

"I want to put something in the cement."

"Like what?"

The small metal box made a racket as she set it on the counter. Brandon opened the lid. "A glove."

"From the first time we met."

He nodded. "Tennis ball — from batting practice."

She peered into the box. "Sand from our morning jogs on the beach."

"And a rock?"

She touched the water-washed stone reverently. "From the creek where you found me. Because Christ is the Solid Rock of our relationship, and no other foundation will do."

Satin rustled, and Brandon couldn't wipe the grin from his face even if he wanted to. His bride was the most beautiful woman in the world. The answer to his prayers, gift-wrapped in satin and lace, let go of his hands after they'd exchanged vows and wedding bands. Brandon helped Della kneel at the altar. Her snowy gown flowed behind her, and the veil softened his view of her face. He took his place beside her and slid his left arm around her tiny waist. It was all so right — this special closeness they felt as their pastor prepared to serve them Holy Communion.

They'd had premarital counseling, and he'd developed a whole new view of marriage. This would be the first time he and Della would break bread together as man and wife. Sharing the Lord's cup held deep significance — God was the center of their marriage. Through Him, the two of them became one.

Hands and heart joined, they finally rose

and turned to one another. Lifting her veil gave him a rush of joy. Love lit her eyes, and the kiss they shared was the sweetest thing in his life.

"Ladies and gentlemen," Pastor MacIntosh said, "I'd like to introduce you to Mr. and Mrs. Brandon Stevens."

Vanessa was Della's matron of honor. She hastily gave the bouquet back to Della, and Brandon tucked Della's hand into the crook of his arm. He led her up the aisle, out of the church, and on to the bright future God had given them.

ABOUT THE AUTHOR

Cathy Marie Hake is a Southern California native who loves her work as a nurse and Lamaze teacher. She and her husband have a daughter, a son, and three dogs, so life is never dull or quiet. Cathy considers herself a sentimental packrat, collecting antiques and Hummel figurines. In spare moments, she reads, bargain hunts, and makes a huge mess with her new hobby of scrapbooking.